The Circassian Slave

Maturin Murray Ballou

THE CIRCASSIAN SLAVE:

OR, THE SULTAN'S FAVORITE.

A Story of Constantinople and the Caucasus.

BY

LIEUTENANT MURRAY.

1851.

PUBLISHER's NOTE.—The following Novelette was originally published in THE PICTORIAL DRAWING ROOM COMPANION, and is but a specimen of the many deeply entertaining Tales, and the gems of literary merit, which grace the columns of that elegant and highly popular journal. THE COMPANION embodies a corps of contributors of rare literary excellence, and is regarded as the ne plus ultra, by its scores of thousands of readers.

PREFACE.

The following story relates to that exceedingly interesting and romantic portion of the world bordering on the Black Sea, the Sea of Marmora, and the Bosphorus. The period of the story being quite modern, its scenes are a transcript of the present time in the city of the Sultan. The peculiarities of Turkish character are of the follower of Mahomet, as they appear to-day; and the incidents depicted are such as have precedents daily in the oriental capital. Leaving the tale to the kind consideration of the reader, the author would not fail to express his thanks for former indulgence and favor.

CHAPTER I.

THE SLAVE MARKET.

Upon one of those hot, sultry summer afternoons that so often prevail about the banks of the Bosphorus, the sun was fast sinking towards its western course, and gilding as it went, the golden crescents of a thousand minarets, now dancing with fairy feet over the rippling waters of Marmora, now dallying with the spray of the oarsmen's blades, as they pulled the gilded caique of some rich old Mussulman up the tide of the Golden Horn. The soft and dainty scented air came in light zephyrs off the shore of Asia to play upon the European coast, and altogether it was a dreamy, siesta-like hour hat reigned in the Turkish capital.

Let the reader come with us at this time into the circular area that forms the slave market of Constantinople. The bazaar is well filled; here are Egyptians, Bulgarians, Persians, and even Africans; but we will pass them by and cross to the main stand, where are exposed for sale some score of Georgians and Circassians. They are all chosen for their beauty of person, and present a scene of more than usual interest, awaiting the fate that the future may send them in a kind or heartless master; and knowing how much of their future peace depends upon this chance, they watch each new comer with almost painful interest as he moves about the area.

A careless crowd thronged the place, lounging about in little knots here and there, while one lot of slave merchants, with their broad but graceful turbans, were sitting round a brass vessel of coals, smoking or making their coffee, and discussing the matters pertaining to their trade. Some came there solely to smoke their opium-drugged pipes, and some to purchase, if a good bargain should offer and a beauty be sold cheap. Here were sprightly Greeks, sage Jews, and moody Armenians, but all outnumbered by the sedate old Turks, with beards sweeping their very breasts. It was a motley crowd that thronged the slave market.

Now and then there burst forth the ringing sound of laughter front an enclosed division of the place where were confined a whole bevy of Nubian damsels, flat-nostriled and curly-headed, but as slight and fine-limbed as blocks of polished ebony. They were lying negligently about, in postures that would have taken a painter's eye, but we have naught to do with then at this time.

The females that were now offered for sale were principally of the fair and rosy-cheeked Circassian race, exposed to the curious eve of the throng only so far as delicacy would sanction, yet leaving enough visible to develope charms that fired the spirits of the Turkish crowd; and the bids ran high on this sale of humanity, until at last a beautiful creature, with a form of ravishing loveliness, large and lustrous eyes, and every belonging that might go to make up a Venus, was led forth to the auctioneer's stand. She was young and surpassingly handsome, while her hearing evinced a degree of modesty that challenged their highest admiration.

Of course the bidding was spirited and liberal for such a specimen of her race; but suddenly the auctioneer paused, and declared that he had forgotten to mention one matter which might, perhaps, be to some purchasers even a favorable consideration, which was, that the slave was deaf and dumb! The effects of this announcement were of course various; on some it did have a favorable effect, inasmuch as it seemed to add fresh interest to the undoubted charms she evinced, but other shrank back disappointed that a creature of so much loveliness should be even partially bereft of her faculties.

"Are you deaf and dumb?" asked an old Turk, approaching the Circassian where she stood, as though he wished to satisfy himself as to the truth of what the salesman had announced.

The slave lifted her eyes at his approach, and only shook her head in signification that she could not speak, as she saw his lips move in the utterance of some words, which she supposed addressed to her. The splendid beauty of her eyes, and the general expression of her countenance, seemed to act like magic on the Musselman, who, turning to the auctioneer, bid five hundred piasters, a hundred advance on the first offer.

At this moment a person wearing the uniform of the Turkish navy, made his way towards the stand from the centre of the bazaar, where he had for some minutes been intently regarding the scene, and bid

"Six hundred piasters."

"Seven," said the previous bidder.

"Eight," continued the naval officer.

"Eight fifty," responded the old Turk.

"Nine hundred," said the officer, with a promptness that attracted the attention of the crowd.

"One thousand piasters," said his competitor, as he continued to regard her exquisite and beautiful mould, and her features, so like a picture, in their regular and artistic lines of beauty. It was very plain that the old Turk felt, as he gazed upon her, so silent yet so beautiful, that she was richly worth her weight in pearls.

"A thousand piasters," repeated the vender of the slave market, turning once more to the officer, then added, as he received no encouraging sign from him, "a thousands piasters, and sold!"

The officer regarded her with much interest, and turned away in evident disappointment, for the old Turk who had outbid him, had gone beyond any means that he possessed. The purchaser handed forth the money in a couple of small bags, and throwing a close veil over the head of the slave, led her away through the narrow and winding streets of old Stamboul to the water's side, where they entered a caique that awaited them, and pulled up the harbor.

Its shooting caiques, its forest of merchantmen, and its hoard of Turkish war ships; were changed, in a few moments of swift pulling, for the breathless solitude of the Valley of Sweet Waters, which opens with a gentle curve from the Golden Horn, and winds away into the hills towards Belgrade, where the river assumes the character of a silvery stream, threading its way through a soft and verdant meadow on either hand, as beautiful in aspect as the Prophet's Paradise. The spot where the Sultan sends his swift-footed Arabians to graze on the earliest verdure that decks the face of spring.

It was up this fairy-like passage that the dumb slave was swept in her master's caique, and by scenes so beautiful as even to enchant her sad and silent bosom. The Turk marked well the influence of the scenery upon the Circassian, and slowly stroked his beard with silent satisfaction at the sight.

The caique soon stopped before a gorgeous palace, in the midst of this fine plain, and the Turk, by a signal, summoned the guard of eunuchs from a tent of the Prophet's green, that was pitched near the banks of the Barbyses, that ran its meandering course through this verdant scene. It was a princely home, the proudest harem in all this gem of the Orient, for the old Turk had acted not for himself in the purchase he had made, but as the agent of a higher will than his own, and the dumb slave was led to the seraglio of the Sultan.

The old Turk was evidently a privileged body, and following close upon the heels of the eunuchs, he divested himself of his slippers at the entrance of the palace, and led the slave before the "Brother of the Sun."

The monarch was a noble specimen of his race, tall, commanding, and with a spirit of firmness breathing from his expressive face. His beard was jetty black, and gave a much older appearance to his features than belonged to them. He was the child of a seraglio, whose mothers were chosen for beauty alone, and how could he escape being handsome? The blood of Circassian upon Circassian was in his veins, and the trace of their nationality was upon his brow, but there was in the eye a doomed darkness of expression that caused the beautiful creature before him to almost tremble with fear.

"Beautiful, indeed," mused the Sultan, as he gazed upon the slave with undisguised interest; "and how much did she cost us, good Mustapha?"

"One thousand piasters, excellency" answered the agent, with profound respect.

"A thousand piasters," repeated the monarch, again gazing at the slave.

"Yes, excellency, the bids ran high."

"A goodly sum, truly, Mustapha, but a goodly return," continued the Sultan.

"There was one fault, excellency," continued the agent, "that I feared might disappoint you."

"And what is that, good Mustapha?"

"She is both deaf and dumb, excellency."

"A mute?"

"Yes, excellency."

"Both deaf and dumb," repeated the Sultan, rising from his divan and approaching the lovely Circassian, actuated by the interest that he felt at so singular an announcement.

While the old Turk stroked his beard with an air of satisfaction at the result of his purchase as it regarded the approval of his master, the slave bent humbly before the monarch, for though she knew not by any word or sign addressed to her who her master was, yet she felt that no one could assume that air of dignity and command but the Sultan. A blush stole over the pale face of the Circassian as the monarch laid his hand on her arm and gazed intently upon her face, and whatever his inward thoughts were, his handsome countenance expressed a spirit of tenderness and gentle concern for her situation that became him well, for clemency is the brightest jewel in a crown.

"Deaf and dumb," repeated the Sultan against to himself, "and yet so very beautiful."

"She is beautiful, indeed, excellency," said the old Turk, echoing his master's thoughts.

"So they sought her eagerly at the market, good Mustapha, did they not?"

"Excellency, yes. One of your own officers bid against me heavily; he wore the marine uniform."

"Ha! did the fellow know you?" asked the Sultan, quickly, with a flashing eye that showed how capable that face was of a far different expression from that which the dumb slave had given rise to.

"I think he did not know me, excellency."

After a moment's pause the Sultan turned again to the gentle girl that stood before him, and taking her hand, endeavored by his looks of kind assurance to express to her that he should strive to make her happy; and as he smoothed her dark, glossy hair tenderly, the slave bent her forehead to the hand that held her own, in token of gratitude for the kindness with which she was received, and when she raised her face again. Both the Sultan and Mustapha saw that tears had wet her cheeks, and her bosom heaved quickly with the emotion that actuated her.

At this moment the Circassian felt her dress slightly drawn from behind, and turning, confronted the person of a lad who might, judging from his size, be some seventeen years of age. His form was beautiful in its outline, and his step light and graceful; but the face, alas! that throne of the intellect was a barren waste, and his vacant eye and lolling lip showed at once that the poor boy was little less than an idiot. And yet, as he looked upon the slave, and saw the tear glistening in her eye, there seemed to be a flash of intelligence cross his features, as though there was still a spark of heaven in the boy. But 'twas gone again, and seeming to forget the object that had led him to her side, he sank down upon the cushioned floor, and played with a golden tassel as an infant would char have done.

The idiot was an exemplification of a strange but universal superstition among the Turks. With these eastern people there is a traditionary belief in what is called the evil eye, answering to the evil spirit that is accredited to exist by more civilized nations. Any human being bereft of reason, or seriously deformed in any way, is held by them to be a protection against the blight of the evil eye, which, being once cast upon a person, renders him doomed forever. Holding, therefore, that dwarfs, idiots or mad-men are partially inspired, every considerable such establishment supports one or more, whose privilege it is to follow, untrammeled, their own pleasure. The idiot boy, in the Sultan's palace, was one of this class, whom no one thwarted, and who was regarded with a half superstitious reverence by all.

While this scene had been transpiring between the idiot boy and the slave, the Sultan had been talking with Mustapha concerning the latter. It seemed by his story that she had been very ill since she was brought from her native valley, and that she was hardly yet recovered from the debility that had followed her sickness. She would not write nor read one word of either the Turkish or Circassian tongue, and therefore could only express herself by signs; for which reason, neither those who sold her nor the purchaser knew aught of her history beyond the fact that she was a Circassian, and also that she seemed to be less happy than those of her countrywomen generally who come to Constantinople. This might be owing to the affliction under which she labored as to being dumb, but it was evident that Sultan Mahomet thought otherwise as he gazed silently at her.

"She came not of her own free will from her native vales, Mustapha," said his master.

"No one knows, excellency, though her people generally come most cheerfully to our harems."

"There is no means of understanding her save by signs?" asked the Sultan.

"None, excellency."

"Take her to the harem, Mustapha," said his master, after a few moments of thoughtful silence, "take her to the harem, and give strict charge that she be well cared for."

"Excellency, yes," said the old Turk, with a profound reverence after the manner of the East, "your wish is your slave's law," he continued, as he turned away.

"And look you, good Mustapha," said the Sultan, recalling him once more, "say it is our will that she be made as happy as may be."

"Excellency, yes," again repeated the old man with a salaam, and then turning to the Circassian, he signed to her to follow him.

As the slave retired she could not but look back at the Sultan, who had greeted her with such kind consideration, and as she did so she met his dark, piercing eye bent upon her in gentle pity. She almost sighed to leave the presence of one who had showed her the first kindness, the first token of thoughtful consideration for her situation since she left her own home, far away beyond the sea. But Mustapha beckoned her forward, and she hastened to obey his summons, wondering as she went what was to be her fate; whether that was to be her future home, and what position she was to hold there. Musing thus, she followed the Turk towards the sacred precincts of the harem.

The monarch left alone, save the thoughtless boy, who lay upon the rich divan, coiled up like an animal gone to sleep, seemed to be troubled in his mind. Stern and imperious by nature, it was not usual for him to evince such feeling as had exercised him towards the dumb slave, and it was plain that his heart was moved by feelings that were novel there. Touching a silver gong that hung pendent from the wall, just within reach of his arm, a Nubian slave opened the hangings of the apartment, and appeared as though he had come out of the wall.

The slave knew well his master's summons, and preparing for him the bowl of his pipe, and lighting it, coiled the silken tube to his hand, and on his knee presented the amber mouthpiece.

Thus occupied, the Sultan was soon lost in the dreamy narcotic of the tobacco.

CHAPTER II.

THE SULTAN'S HAREM.

The harem into which the dumb Circassian girl was conducted by the woman to whom the old Turk delivered his message, was a place of such luxuriant splendor as to puzzle her, and she stood like one amazed for some moments.—The costly and grateful lounges, the heavy and downy carpets, the rich velvet and silken hangings about the walls, the picturesque and lovely groups of female slaves that laughed and toyed with each other, mingling in pleasant games, the rich though scanty dress of these favorites of the Sultan, all were confusing and dazzling to her untutored eye, and when, after a few moments' minutes, a dozen of these lovely girls crowded about her with curious eyes to know who was the new comer that was to be their companion, the poor girl shrunk back half abashed, for she could not speak to them.

They too were puzzled that she made no reply to them, and stood there in wonder.

It was only for a moment, however, when the beautiful stranger pointed to her mouth and ears significantly, and gently shook her head with a sadness of expression that was electrical, for each one instantly understood her meaning, and pitied her. Some little feeling of envy might have been ready to burst forth in the breasts of those about her, but gentle pity loves to linger by beauty's side, and so they all loved and condoled with the fair stranger. One took her hand and led her to a cushion in the centre of the little circle that had just been formed, another unloosed the wealth of beautiful hair that astonished them by its dark richness and profusion as it fell about her fair neck. She who had unloosed the new comer's hair, now fell to braiding it in solid masses and plaiting it about her head.

A second one taking a rare bracelet of pearls off her own fair arms, placed it upon the Circassian's, and sealed it there with a kiss!— Another removed the leather shoes she wore, and replaced them with satin ones of curious workmanship and richly wrought with thread of gold, and still another loosened the coarse mantle that enshrouded her shoulders, and covered her with a shawl that had come across the desert from the far east, rich in texture and beautiful as costly. And as another tossed a handful of fresh flowers into her lap, the poor girl's cheeks became wet with tears, for their unselfish kindness and generous tenderness had touched heart.

But these tokens were quickly brushed away and kisses took their place, while fair and delicate hands were busy upon her, until the poor slave who had so lately stood exposed in the open bazaar of the capital, now saw among this family of the Turkish monarch, literally as a star of the harem. In beauty, she did indeed outshine them all, but they forgot this in the memory of her misfortune, and envied not the dumb slave. They touched her fingers with henna dye, and anointed her with rare and costly perfumes, seeming to vie with each other in their interesting efforts to deck and beautify one who had only the voluptuous softness of her dark eyes to thank them with, for those lovely lips, of such tempting freshness in their coral hue, could utter no sound.

They brought to her all their jewels and rich ornaments to amuse her, and each one contributed to give her from out their store some becoming ornament, now a diamond broach, and now a ruby ring, next a necklace of emeralds, interspersed with glowing opals, a fourth added a girdle of golden chain braced at every link by close and richly cut garnets, and other rings of sapphire and amethysts, until the lovely stranger was dazzling with the combined brilliancy and reflection of so many rare and beautiful jewels about her person.

It was not the jewels that so gratified the young Circassian, but the good will they represented. She cared little for them intrinsically, beautiful and rich as they were, but she grew very fast to love the donors.

Days passed on in this manner, and the Sultan was no less surprised than delighted to witness this voluntary kindness and affection that was so freely rendered to the lovely girl. Her affliction seemed to render her sacred in his eyes, and there was no kindness on his part that was forgotten. Her manners and intelligent bearing showed her to belong to the better class of her own nation, and her gentle dignity commanded respect as well as love. She had already come to a degree of understanding with those about her that was sufficient as it regarded her ordinary wishes and wants, but of the past or future she had not means to communicate, her tongue was sealed, and for this reason her history must remain a hidden mystery to those about her whom she loved, and would gladly have confided in.

One occupation seemed to delight her above all else, it was so simple and beautiful, besides which it enabled her to convey her feelings by means of an agency that, as far as it went, supplied to her the loss of her speech. It was the arranging of flowers so as to make them speak the language of her heart to another, a means of communication in which the women of the East excel. Indeed it is the only mode in which they can hold silent converse, since they know not the cunning of the pen. Engaged in this gentle and pleasing occupation, the Circassian passed hours and days in the study and practice of the sweet language of flowers.

For hours together, while she was thus occupied, the idiot boy would sit and watch her movements, and now and then receive some kindly token of consideration from her hand that seemed to delight him beyond measure. He followed her every movement with his eye, and seemed only content when close by her side, sitting near her, patient and silent; in fact he could utter but few audible sounds, and no one had ever taught the poor idiot how to talk.

One afternoon, in the gardens that opened from the harem, the Circassian had been engaged thus, sitting beneath the projecting roof of a lattice-work summer house. The sun as it crept down towards the western horizon threw lengthened shadows across the soft green sward where minaret, cypress, or projecting angle of the palace intervened. The boy would pick out one of those dark shadows, and sitting down where it terminated, seem to think that he could keep it there, but when the shadow lengthened every moment more and more, and seemed to his untutored and simple comprehension to creep out from under him, he would look amazed to see how it was done while he sat upon it.

In following up a projecting shadow thus, he had come at last almost to the very side of the dumb slave just as a gaudy winged parrot lit upon the eve of the summer house on a large piece of the picket work that had been used as an ornament for its top, but which having been broken from its position, had slid down to the very eaves and now hung but half suspended upon the roof. Even the lighting of the parrot upon its edge was sufficient to balance it from the fragile support that retained it on the roof, and then it slid off immediately above the head of the Circassian girl.

The boy was on his feet as quick as thought itself, and springing to the spot, with both hands outspread above her head, he canted the heavy frame work away from her so that it came upon the ground, sinking deep into the earth from its sharp points and considerable weight. Had the falling mass come upon her head, as it would most inevitably have done but for the boy, its effect must have been instantly fatal. The Circassian saw the imminent service the boy had rendered her, but he was sitting on the end of another shadow in a moment after!

Was it reason or instinct that had caused him to make that successful effort with such wonderful speed and accuracy? The slave looked at him in wonder. It was very evident that he had already forgotten the service which he had rendered, and the same listless, childlike, and almost idiotic expression was in his face. this event endeared the boy very much to the Circassian, and she never failed to show him every kindness in her power. She would arrange his straggling dress, and part his hair, smoothly away from his handsome forehead, and give him always of each delicacy provided for herself, until the boy seemed to feel himself almost solely dependent upon her, and to seek her side as a faithful hound might have done.

Thus had time passed with the dumb slave in the Sultan's palace on the Barbyses.

At times she would stroll among the rare beds of plants, and culling fresh chaplets for her head, wreathe herself a fragrant garland, ever finding some familiar scent that recalled her far off home in all its freshness. Wearied of this she wandered among the jasper fountains, and watched the play of those waters, the soft and rippling music of which she might not hear, or still further on in the many labyrinths of the garden and harem walks, would throw herself upon some rich cushions beside a silver urn, where burnt sweet aloes and sandal wood and rods of spice to perfume the air. At early morn she loved to pet the blue pigeons that had been brought from far off Mecca, held so sacred by the faithful, to feed them from her own hands, and to toy with the golden thrushes from Hindostan, and the gaudy birds of Paradise that flew about with other rare and beautiful songsters in this fairy palace of the Sultan.

Her companions watching her with loving eyes, never faltered in their kindness and love for her. Indeed it seemed as though they could not avoid tendering her this affection, she was so very beautiful and gentle in all things. They had named her Lalla, or the tulip, because of her love for that beautiful and delicate flower.

The Sultan looked upon the young Circassian—she had numbered hardly seventeen summers—more in the light of a daughter than a slave, and she who could have feared him else, even looked with pleasure for his coming, and sought in a thousand earnest but silent ways to please him. There was no spirit of sycophancy in this, no coquetry, or false pretense; she was all simpleness and truth, and her conduct towards her master sprang alone from a sense of gratitude. Thus too did the monarch translate her behaviour to him, for he was well versed in human nature, young as he was, and could appreciate the promptings of a young and trusting spirit, such as she exhibited in all her intercourse with him.

As exhibited in our illustration, the Sultan would often seek her side in the harem, his tall, manly form contrasting strongly with her gentle and delicate proportions, and he would regard her thus with tender solicitude, too fully realizing her misfortune not to pity and respect her, and he felt too that these frequent meetings were binding his heart in a tender bondage to her. Sultan Mahomet was a fine specimen of a Turk; in features he was markedly handsome, and his long, flowing beard gave to him the appearance of more age than was rightfully his. His physical developments were manly, and to look upon he was "every inch a king." Lalla was no less beautiful as a female; indeed she was far handsomer as it related to such a comparison, and those who saw them so often together in the harem could not but think what a noble pair they were, and seemingly worthy of each other.

She possessed all that soft delicacy of appearance that reminds the sterner sex how frail and dependent is woman, while she bore in her face that sweet and winning expression of intellect, that, in other climes more favored by civilization, and where cultivation adds so much to the charms of her sex, would alone have marked her as beautiful. Her eyes, which were surpassing in their dreamy loveliness, were enhanced in beauty by a languid plaintiveness that a realizing sense of her misfortunes had imparted to the expression of her face, while her whole manner bore that subdued and quiet air that sorrow ever imparts. Those of her companions who knew her best, could easily understand that her heart was far away from her present home; for her actions spoke this as plainly as might have ever been done by words, and poor Lalla, wherever she had come from, and under whatever circumstances, had evidently left her heart behind her among her childhood's scenes.

The Sultan was earnestly interested in his dumb but beautiful slave, and instituted a series of inquiries as to her history. His agents were instructed to find out, if possible, the mode in which she had been brought hither, and also to learn, if possible, the manner and cause of her leaving her native hills in the Caucasus; for of these things the fair girl had no means of communicating. The monarch and all Constantinople knew that her people generally looked forward with joy to the time when they should be old enough to be taken to the Turkish capital, and seek their fortunes there, and the fact of this being so different apparently with Lalla, created the more curiosity to ferret out her story.

But all their efforts were useless in the pursuit of this purpose. Since the Sultan's object in the inquiry was announced, much time had transpired; but had his proclamation met the eye or ear of those who transported the fair Circassian hither, they would hardly have responded to it, as it might, for aught they knew, cost them their heads. And thus the gentle slave lived on, a mystery to those about her which even she was unable to solve.

"You made all inquiries at the bazaar, good Mustapha?" asked the Sultan.

"Most rigid inquiries, excellency."

"And could learn nothing of the history of this beautiful slave?" continued the Sultan.

"Nothing, excellency."

"It is very strange that no one can be found who knows aught about her. Did you trace her back to those who sold her to the salesman of the bazaar?"

"Yes, excellency, and two sales beyond that; but it seemed that although so beautiful, the fact of her being dumb had caused her to be very much undervalued, and she had passed through the hands of a number of irresponsible slave merchants, who took but little heed of her before she came to the bazaar."

"Doubtless, then, we may hardly expect to hear more concerning her."

"The reward you offered was munificent, excellency, but has brought no response."

"You have not yet purchased for me those Georgians, good Mustapha," continued the monarch, after a few moments' pause, and probably desiring to change a subject in which he felt that he was only too much interested.

"Excellency, they are held at so high a price that I have refused to pay it."

"Well, well, be discreet, and purchase shrewdly," said the Sultan, resuming his pipe.

And in this manner the Sultan forgot his lovely slave, and removing the mouth-piece of his pipe now and then, continued to question his slave touching the matters that seemed to pertain to his department of the household.

Poor Lalla! she had only her own unhappiness to brood upon as she sat by some rippling fountain and watched its silvery jets and sparkling drops, at times forgetting for a moment her sadness of heart in the beauty that completely surrounded her; and then again, perhaps mingling her tears with the fragrant blossoms that strewed her lap and filled her hands. Alas! poor child! how it would have eased the quick beating of thy heart if thou couldst have told the story of thy unhappiness to some other confiding spirit.

The idiot boy would watch these tears, and at times he would wear a fixed, vacant stare, as though he took no note of their meaning; and at others, he would seem to comprehend their sorrowful import. When this was the case, he would creep close to her side and lay his head by her feet, and closing his eyes, remain as motionless as death. This would at length arouse her from her unhappy mood, and she would turn and gently caress the poor boy. Once when she had done this, she saw a large tear drop steal out from beneath his closed eyelids, and fall across his check. She rejoiced at this, for, while all others set him down as without feeling, she saw that kindness at least would awaken his heart.

Lalla had been weeping, and now sat alone by a bed of fragrant flowers, when one of those fairy-like children of the harem, scarcely older than herself, came tripping with light and thoughtless steps towards her, and detecting her saddened mood, kissed way the tears that still lingered upon her cheeks, and binding a wreath of fresh and beautiful flowers about her head, lay down in Lalla's lap and toyed with the stray buds, looking up into her eyes with gentle love and tenderness.

How grateful were these delicate and beautiful manifestations of feeling to the lonely-hearted slave.

CHAPTER III.

THE BEDOUIN ARABS.

It was one of those soft days, made up of nature's sweetest smiles, of sunshine and gentle zephyrs, when sky, and sea, and shore were radiant, and all the earth seemed glad, that a lone horseman sat with the reins cast loosely upon the arching neck of his proud Arabian, on the plain beyond the Armenian cemetery, in the suburbs of Constantinople. The rider was dressed in the plainest attire of a quiet citizen, though the material of his clothes and the few ornaments that were visible about his person indicated their owner to be one who was no meagre possessor of the riches of this world. Both rider and horse were as still as though they had been carved in marble instead of being living objects, save the quick, nervous motion, now and then, of the full-blooded animal's ears, as some distant sound rose over the Turkish city.

The Mussulman, as he sat there in a thoughtful and silent mood, stroked slowly the jetty black beard that swept his breast, while he seemed completely absorbed in contemplating the scene before him. He had galloped at once from paved streets to the unfenced and uncultivated desert that stretches away from the seven hills of Stamboul to the very horizon. No wonder he paused there to gaze upon the beauties that the eye might take in at a single glance.

Before him lay the city in all its oriental beauty, while, on every sloping hillside about it, in every rural nook stood a dark nekropolis, or city of the dead, shadowed by the close growing cypresses, beneath whose shadows turbaned heads alone are permitted to rest. From out of these, stretching its slender point away towards the blue heavens, rose the fairy-like minaret, as if pointing whither had gone the spirits of the faithful.

There, too, lay the incomparable Bosphorus, stretching away towards the sea, and the beautiful isles in the sweet waters of Marmora, with countless boats swarming in the Golden Horn, and then the eye would turn back again to the city with its thousand minarets. There lay, too, the velvet-carpeted Valley of Sweet Waters, where was the Sultan's serai, looking like some fair scene described in the Koran, so soft, fairy-like, and enticing.

The rider now slowly gathered up the reins from his horse's neck, and. slightly restraining the spirited animal by a pressure of the curb, permitted him slowly to walk on while his master appeared still to be lost in thought. Once or twice he cast his eyes again towards the city, and then again mused to himself, as though his cares and thoughts lay there. So much was the rider absorbed within himself that he did not observe two power Bedouin Arabs of the desert, who had wandered to the outskirts of the city, and whose longing eyes were bent, not on him, but upon the horse which he rode. To the skillful eyes of these children of the desert he was almost invaluable; every step betrayed his metal, while the clean limb, nervous action, and distended nostrils told of the fleetness that was in him!

You may trust an Arab often with gold or precious goods; the very fact of the confidence, you accord to him makes him faithful. You may trust your life in his hands, and the laws of hospitality shall protect you; but trust him not with a fine horse—that will betray him, though nothing else might do so. Born in the desert where they are reared and loved so well, he imbibes from childhood a regard for the full blooded barb, that falls little short of reverence; and being once possessed of one, no money can part them. The two Bedouins stealthily watched the Turk as he rode slowly along, and were evidently only awaiting a favorable moment to attack and overcome him.

By an ingenious movement they doubled a slight hillock that lay between them and the woods of Belgrade, and as they came up on the other side, placed themselves directly in the path of the horseman. Still they were unobserved by him, and not until one had laid his hand upon the bridle, and the other violent hands upon his garments, did he arouse from the dreamy thoughts which had so completely absorbed him. Thus taken at disadvantage, the horseman was forced from the saddle before he could offer any resistance, but having once reached the ground, and being fairly on his feet, his bright blade glistened in the sun and flashed before the eyes of the Arab robbers.

"Yield us the horse and go thy way!" said one of the assailants, soothingly.

"By the Prophet, never!" shouted the Turk, setting upon them fiercely as he spoke and wounding one severely at the very outset, while he held the bridle of the horse.

The horseman was one used to the weapon he wielded, and the Arabs saw that they had no easy enemy to conquer. He who held the horse was forced to unloose the bridle to defend himself, while the other was now striving to use the gun that was strapped to his back; but they were at too close quarters for the employing of such a weapon, and the stout, iron-like frames of the Arabs were fast conquering the skill and endurance of the Turk. But that bright sword was not wielded so skillfully for naught, and one of the robbers was already glad to creep from without its reach, just as his companion succeeded in breaking the finely-tempered blade with his gun barrel, leaving the Turk comparatively at his mercy; and again he bade him surrender the horse, the animal trained to the nicest point of perfection, still remaining quiet close to the spot where the encounter had taken place. The clashing of the weapons had startled him, and he breathed quick, and his ears showed that the nervous energy of his frame was aroused, but a spear point thrust into his very flanks would not have started him away until his master bade him to go.

"Yield thou now, or die!" shouted the excited Bedouin, drawing his long dagger.

"By the Prophet, never!" again exclaimed the Turk, with vehemence, though he panted sorely from the extraordinary exertion he had made to defend himself from the attack of his two assailants.

All this had transpired in far less time than we have occupied in the relation, and once more now having him greatly at disadvantage, the Bedouins rushed upon him.

But there came now upon the scene a third party, at this excited moment, from out the forest of Belgrade. He seemed but a weary traveller, though when his eyes rested upon the scene we have described, an instantaneous change came over him, and he appeared at once to comprehend the meaning of the whole affair. Just at the very moment when the Arab, who had been partially vanquished and somewhat severely wounded, regained his feet, and was coming once more to the contest, the traveller, espousing the side of the weaker party, who was now indeed unarmed, fiercely attacked the robbers with a heavy staff that he carried, and in a moment, being comparatively fresh, and aided by the surprise as well as the lusty blows that he dealt about him, he caused the two Bedouins to retreat precipitately, though they made a last and nearly successful effort to carry off the horse, but this the ready arm of the traveller prevented.

A moment sufficed to put both the Turk and his deliverer in breath once more.

"Who art thou that hast been so opportunely sent to rescue me?" asked the Turk, at he called his horse by his name, and the beautiful animal came quietly to his side.

"A poor traveller, well nigh wearied by the long way," answered the other.

"Thy habiliments bespeak thee as coming from the North, and they look as though want had been thy companion on the way," continued he whom the traveller had rescued.

"It has, indeed," said the other; "fatigue and want have kept me company these many long days." As he answered thus, he wiped the perspiration that his late exertion had caused, from his brow.

"I owe you my hearty thanks for this timely service," said the Turk.

"A trifling deed that any man in my place would have performed."

"Take this," replied the Turk, depositing a purse, heavy with gold, in the stranger's hands. "Use the contents as you will, and when you have need of further assistance, if there be aught that one possessing some influence can serve thee in, present that purse at the gates of the seraglio gardens, and you will find me."

"Thanks! a thousand thanks!" said the stranger, "though I must look upon this as a gift, a charity, not in the light of a payment. The service I have rendered might have been afforded by the meanest slave."

"I know well how to esteem a favor, and how to pay it," answered the Turk, as he mounted his spirited horse and turned his head towards the entrance of the city of Constantine. He rode with a free rein now, and the horse dashed over the level plain like an antelope, while his rider sat in the saddle like a Marmaluke.

The traveller poured out a quantity of the gold from the purse to assure himself of its value, and weighing the whole together, said to himself, "A few moments since and I was a beggar, now I am rich; after starving for many long weeks, fortune fills my hand with gold, as if to show me the contrast. It was a piece of singular good luck for me to meet with that rich old Turk; those fellows from the desert were giving him sharp practice; it was only the barb that they wanted. What a cunning eye those rascals have for horseflesh!" Talking thus to himself, he placed the gold in a secure part of his dress, though he need hardly have feared that any one would suspect him of possessing so much of value.

The traveller turned once more to look after the Turk, but he was already far away, though he could still make out his bearing and stately carriage as he disappeared. Picking up the staff that had just served him to such good purpose, he followed in the same path, which would lead him to Constantinople, ere the sun should set in the west.

As he drew nearer to the city he too paused to drink in of the beauties of that twilight hour. The scene was new to him, and his eye was filled with delight and surprise as it roamed over that oriental sunset view. As he came down the side of the gently sloping hill beyond Pera, he paused for a moment in the cemetery there, and among the deep shadows of the heavy funereal cypresses and the tall, white gravestones that thickly overspread the ground, he felt a chill of loneliness that made him to hasten on to a spot where he could catch the last lingering rays of the setting sun kissing the waves of the Bosphorus.

He hurried on now into the city proper, though seemingly without any fixed purpose, and strolled carelessly along, gazing with interest upon all that met his curious eye; now pausing before some rich Persian fountain half as large as a church, covered with curious inscriptions and ornaments of gold; now regarding some sequestered mosque almost hidden in cypresses; and now watching a cluster of indolent-looking, large-trowsered, and moustached, but often handsome men.

Here he was jostled by a bevy of females, shuffling along in their yellow slippers, their faces shrouded to the eyes in that never-forgotten covering with the Turkish wives, the yashmach; now crowded one side by an armed kervos who is clearing the way for some dignitary to follow; and now forced here and there by, Jew, Turk or Armenian. But still, while he regarded intently this busy scene, he yielded the way to all, for he was wearied and his spirits were evidently depressed both by physical and mental suffering.

The traveller was started from his reverie by the attack upon him of some hundred dogs, who saluted his ears with such a volley of howls as nearly to stun him. These natural scavengers are protected by the laws here, and whenever a stranger is seen, one whose dress or manner betrays him as such, they set upon him like mad, but the staff that had stood him in such good service not long before, soon dispersed his canine tormentors, though he showed that even this little circumstance annoyed him seriously; it was a sad welcome to a stranger.

Perhaps there is no feeling more desolate and forsaken in its promptings than that realized by one who finds himself alone in a crowd. His inward solitude is more acutely realized by the contrast he sees about him, and he feels how much he is alone. Thus it was with the young traveller who had made his way into the city as we have described; he was indeed solitary though surrounded by hosts, for he was a stranger and knew no one in the Sultan's beautiful capital.

Still he wandered on amid the crowd until at last he found himself in the drug bazaar, where a scene so peculiarly oriental and rich met his observation as to make him forget for a while his own sad and weary mood. Strange and antique jars of every shape crowded the shelves of the various stalls, their edges turned over with brilliant colored paper, each drug bearing its own appropriate one. The shelves were bending under the weight of rich gums, spices, incense-wood, medicinal roots, and cunning dyes. The sedate Turk who presides over each stall at this hour, sits with his legs crossed and his eyes rolling in a sort of dreamy languor from the powerful narcotic of his opium-drugged pipe. He is happy and thoughtless in the dissipation that sooner or later hurries him to the grave.

It was the corflew hour, and from out the lofty spires of the neighboring mosques there came a voice that called to prayer. Each Mussulman prostrated himself, no matter in what occupation he was engaged, and bowing his head towards Mecca, the tomb of the Prophet, performing his silent devotion. In famine, in pestilence, or in plenty, five times a day the Turk finds time for this solemn religious duty; whether right or wrong in creed, what a lesson it is to the Christian. And so thought the lonely traveller, for he bent his own head upon his breast in respectful awe at the exhibition he beheld.

Pausing in silence until the scene had changed from the solemn act of prayer to that of busy life, he passed out of the dim-lighted bazaar once more into the open street. Night was fast creeping over the city, and he remembered how much he required rest and refreshment, and availing himself of the proffered services of a Jewish interpreter, he told his wants, and not long after found himself seated in one of the little Armenian houses of resort in the outskirts of Stamboul.

Here again he found enough of character to study in the singular and medley company that resorted thither, but wayworn and weary, after partaking of some refreshment, he soon lost himself in sleep.

It was late on the subsequent morning when the traveller awoke, greatly refreshed by his night's rest, and once more refreshing the inner man with meats and such coffee as one gets only in Turkey, he roamed again into the streets, where we must leave him to pursue his purpose, be it what it might, while we turn to other scenes in our story, taking the reader across the sea, to another, hut no loss interesting land.

CHAPTER IV.

VALES OF CIRCASSIA.

Circassia, the land of beauty and oppression, whose noble valleys produce such miracles of female loveliness, and whose level plains are the vivid scenes of such terrible struggles; where a brave, unconquerable peasantry have, for a very long period, defied the combined powers of the whole of Russia, and whose daughters, though the children of such brave sires, are yet taught and reared from childhood to look forward to a life of slavery in a Turkish harem as the height of their ambition—Circassia, the land of bravery, beauty and romance, is one of the least known, but most interesting spots in all Europe.

Whether it be that the genial air of its hills and vales possesses power to beautify the forms and faces of its daughters, or that they inherit those charms from their ancestors by right of blood, we may not say; but from the farthest dates, it has ever supplied the Sultan and his people with the lovely beings who have rendered of the harems of the Mussulmen so celebrated for the charms they enshrine. Its daughters have been n the mothers of the highest dignitaries of the courts, and Sultan Mahomet himself was born of a Circassian mother.

Unendowed with mental culture, Providence has seemed, in a degree, to compensate to the girls of Circassia for want of intellectual brilliancy, by rendering them physically beautiful almost beyond description. No wonder, then, educated, or rather uneducated as they are, that the visions of their childhood, the dreams of their girlish days, and even the aspirations of their riper years, should be in the anticipation of a life of independence, luxury and love, in those fairy-like homes that skirt the Bosphorus at Constantinople.

Being from their earliest childhood taught by their parents to look upon this destiny as an enviable one, these fair girls do not fail to appreciate and fully realize the captivating charms that Heaven has so liberally endowed them with, and wait with trembling breasts and hopeful hearts for the period when they shall change the humble scenes of their existence, from the long and rugged ravines of the

Caucasus, for the glittering and gaudy palaces of the Mussulmen, in the Valley of Sweet Waters, or on the banks of the Golden Horn.

In former years, the Trebizond merchantman took on board his cargo of young and lovely Circassians, and navigated the Black Sea with a flowing sheet and a flag flying at his peak, which told his business and the commerce that he was engaged in; now the trade is contraband, and the slave ship has to pick its way cautiously about the island of Crimea, and keep a sharp lookout to avoid the Russian war steamers that skirt the entire coast, and keep up a never-ceasing blockade from the Georgian shore to the ancient port of Anapa.

This latter place was, for centuries, one of vital importance to the Circassians, being their general depot or rendezvous for the trade between themselves and the ports that lay at the other extreme of the Black Sea. It was the point where they were always sure to find a ready market for their females, receiving as payment in exchange from the Turks, fire-arms, ammunition and gold. But at last the Russians, assuming a virtue that did not actuate them, stormed and took the fort, ostensibly to put a stop to this trade, as opposed to the principles it involved, but in reality to stop the supplies that enabled the brave mountaineers to oppose them so successfully.

In the country lying immediately back of Anapa, there is a succession of hills and vales of surpassing loveliness, presenting the extremes of wild and rugged mountain scenery, joining fertile plains and beautiful valleys, where, among fragrant and luxuriant groves, many a fair creature has grown up to be brought to the slave market and sold for a price. Vales where brave and stalwart youths have been nurtured and taught the dexterous use of arms, being ever educated to look upon the Russians as their natural enemies, and also to believe that any revenge exercised upon their Moscovite neighbors was not only commendable, but holy and just.

In a valley opening towards the north, a short league above the port of Anapa, at the time of our story there dwelt two families, named Gymroc and Adegah. Both these families traced their ancestry back to noble chiefs, who, in the days of Circassian glory and independence, were at the head of large and powerful tribes of their countrymen. These families, from the fact that they were thus descended, were still held by the mountaineers who lived about them in reverence, and their words had double weight in council when important subjects were discussed; and indeed the present head of each was often chosen to lead them on to the almost constantly recurring battles and bloody guerilla contests that transpired between the mountaineers and their enemies, the Russian Cossacks.

The family of Gymroc was blessed with a fair daughter, an only child, who, though living among a people who were so universally endowed with loveliness in their gentler sex, was famed for her transcendent loveliness far and near, and the youths of the neighboring valleys and plains sighed in their hearts to think that the fairest flower in all Circassia was but blooming to shed its ripened fragrance and loveliness in the harem of some dark and bearded Mahometan, to be the toy of some rich and heartless Turk.

One there was among the young mountaineers, Aphiz Adegah, whose whole life and soul seemed bound up in the lovely Komel, as she was called. Neither was more than eighteen; indeed Komel was not so old, for but sixteen full summers had passed over her head. They had grown up together from very childhood, played together, worked together, sharing each other's burthens, and mutually aiding each other; now quietly watching the sheep and goats upon the hillsides, and now working side by side in the fields, content and happy, so they were always together.

Komel was almost too beautiful. With every grace and delicacy of outline that has, for centuries, rendered her sex so famed in her native land, she added also a sweet, natural intelligence, which, though all uncultivated, was yet ever beaming from her eyes, and speaking forth from her face. Her form possessed a most captivating voluptuous fullness, without once trespassing upon the true lines of female delicacy. Her large and lustrous eyes were brilliant yet plaintive, her lips red and full, and the features generally of a delicate Grecian cast. Her hair was of that dark, glossy hue, that defies comparison, and was heavy and luxuriant in its fullness.

Some one has said that no one can write real poetry until he has known the sting of unhappiness; and sure it is that beauty ever lacks that moss-rose finish that tender melancholy throws about it, until it has known what sorrow is. Komel had been called to mourn, and melancholy had thrown about her a gentle glow of plaintiveness, as a grateful angel added another grace to the rose that had sheltered its slumber, by a shroud of moss.

While she was yet but a little child, her only brother, but little older than herself, and whom she loved with all the sisterly tenderness of her young heart, had strayed away from home to the seaside, and been drowned. From that day she had sorrowed for his loss, and even now as memory recalled her early playmate, the tears would dim her eyes, nor did her spirits seem ever entirely free from the grief that had imbued them at her brother's loss. This hue of tender melancholy was in Komel only an additional beauty, as we have said, and lent its witchery to her other charms.

To say that Komel was insensible to all her personal advantages would be unreasonable, and supposing her not possessed of an ordinary degree of perception. She knew that she was fair, nay, that she was more beautiful than any of the youthful companions of her native valley; but whatever others might have anticipated for her, she had never looked forward, as nearly all of her sex do, in Circassia, to a splendid foreign home across the Black Sea. No, no; her young and loving heart had already made its choice of him she had so long and tenderly loved,—him who had stepped in when there was that vacant spot in her heart that her brother's loss had left, and filled it; for he had been both brother and lover to her from the tenderest years of childhood. They had probably thought little upon the subject of their relation to each other, and had said less, until Komel was nearly sixteen, and then it was only in that tender and hopeful strain of a happy future, and that future to be shared by each other.

Aphiz was as noble and generous in spirit as he was handsome in person. Nature had cast him in a sinewy, yet graceful form; his native mountain air and vigorous habits had ripened his physical developments to an early manliness and already had he more than once charged the enemy upon the open plains of his native land. His falchion had glanced in the tide of battle, and his stout arm had dealt many a fatal blow to the Cossack forces, that sought to conquer and possess themselves of all Circassia. It was a stern school for the young mountaineer, and it was well, as he grew up in this manner, that there was always the tender and chastening association before his mind, of his love for the gentle and beautiful girl who had given her young heart into his keeping. He needed such promptings to enable him to combat the rough associations of the camp, and the hardening duty of a soldier in time of war.

It was, therefore, to her side that he came for that true happiness that emanates from the better feelings of the heart; by her side that he enjoyed the quiet but grand scenery of their native hills and valleys, looking, as it were, through each other's eyes at every beauty, either of thought or that lay tangible before them.

Though both Komel and Aphiz had been thrice happy in their constant intercourse in the days of childhood, though those day. so well remembered, had been to them like a pleasant morning filled with song, or the gliding on of a summer stream, and were marked only by truthfulness and peaceful content, still both realized as they now entered upon a riper age of youth, that they were far happier than ever before, that they loved each other better, and all things about them. It is an error to suppose that childhood is the happiest period of life, though philosophers tell us so, for a child's pleasures are like early spring flowers—pretty, but pale, and fleeting, and scentless. The rich and fragrant treasures of the heart are not developed so early; they come with life's summer, and thus it was with these Circassian youths.

Growing up daily and hourly together to that period when love holds strongest sway over the heart, both felt how happily they could kneel before Heaven and be pronounced one and inseparable; but Aphiz was poor and had no home to offer a bride, besides which, the character of the times was sufficient to prevent their more prudent parents from yielding their consent to such an arrangement as their immediate union, though they offered no opposition to their intimacy.

Komel was of such a happy and cheerful disposition at heart that she scattered pleasure always about her, but Aphiz's very love rendered him thoughtful and perhaps at times a little melancholy; for he feared that some future chance might in an unforeseen, way rob him of her who was so ineffably dear to him. He did not exactly fear that Komel's parents would sell her to go to Constantinople, though they were now, since war and pestilence had swept away lands, home and title, poor enough; and yet there was an undefined fear ever acting in his heart as to her he loved. Sometimes when he realized this most keenly, he could not help whispering his forebodings to Komel herself.

"Nay, dear Aphiz," she would say to him, with a gentle smile upon her countenance, "let not that shadow rest upon thy brow, but rather look with the sun on the bright side of everything. Am I not a simple and weak girl, and yet I am cheerful and happy, while thou, so strong, so brave and manly, art ever fearing some unknown ill."

"Only as it regards thee, Komel, do I fear anything."

"That's true, but I should inspire thee with joy, not fear and uneasiness."

"It is only the love I bear thee, dearest, that makes me so jealous, so anxious, so fearful lest some chance should rob me of thee forever," he would reply tenderly.

"It is ever thus; what is there to fear, Aphiz?"

"I know not, dearest. No one feared your gentle brother's loss years ago, and yet one day he woke happy and cheerful, and went forth to play, but never came back again."

"You speak too truly," answered the beautiful girl with a sigh, "and yet because harm came to him, it is no reason that it should come to me, dear Aphiz."

"Still the fear that aught may happen to separate us is enough to make me sad, Komel."

"Father says, that it is troubles which never happen that chiefly make men miserable," answered the happy-spirited girl, as she laid her head pleasantly upon Aphiz's arm.

They stood at her father's door in the closing hour of the day when they spoke thus, and hardly had Aphiz's words died upon his lips when the attention of both was directed towards the heavy, dark form of a mountain-hawk, as it swept swiftly through the air, and poising itself for an instant, marked where a gentle wood dove was perched upon a projecting bough in the valley. Komel laid her hand with nervous energy upon Aphiz's arm. The hawk was beyond the reach of his rifle, and realizing this he dropped its breach once more to his side. A moment more and the bolder bird was bearing its prey to its mountain nest, there to feed upon it innocent body. Neither Komel nor Aphiz uttered one word, but turned sadly away from the scene that had seemed so applicable to the subject of their conversation. He bade her a tender good night, but as the young mountaineer wended his way down the valley he was sad at heart, and asked himself if Komel might not be that dove.

So earnestly was he impressed with this idea, after the conversation which had just occurred, that twice he turned his steps and resolved to seek the lofty cliff where the hawk had flown, as though he could yet release the poor dove; then remembering himself, he would once more press the downward path to the valley.

It was not to be presumed that Komel should not have found other admirers among the youths of her native valley. She had touched the hearts of many, though being no coquette, they soon learned to forget her, seeing how much her heart was already another's. This, we say, was generally the case, but there was one exception, in the person of a young man but little older than Aphiz, whose name was Krometz. He had loved Komel truly, had told her so, and had been gently refused her own affection by her; but still he persevered, until the love he had borne her had turned to something very unlike love, and he resolved in his heart that if she loved not him, neither should she marry Aphiz.

At one time when Aphiz was in the heat of battle, charging upon the Russian infantry, suddenly he staggered, reeled and fell, a bullet had passed into his chest near the heart. His comrades raised him up and brought him off the battle-field, and after days of painful suffering he recovered, and was once more as well as ever, little dreaming that the bullet which had so nearly cost him his life came from one of his own countrymen. Could the ball have been examined, it would have fitted exactly Krometz's rifle!

Though the rifle shot had failed, Krometz's enmity had in no way abated; he only watched for an opportunity more successfully to effect the object that now seemed to be the motive of his life. Before Komel he was all gentleness, and affected the highest sense of honor, but at heart he was all bitterness and revenge.

Another chapter will show the treacherous and deep game that the rejected lover played.

CHAPTER V.

THE SLAVE SHIP.

It was on a fair summer's evening that a beautiful English built craft, after having beat up the Black Sea all day against the ever prevailing a north-cast wind, now gathered in her light sails and barely kept steerageway by still spreading her jib and mainsail. With the setting sun the breeze had lulled also to rest, and there was but a cap full now coming from off the mountains of the Caucasus, just enough to keep the little clipper steady in hand.

It would be difficult to define the exact class to which the rig of this craft would make her belong, there was so much that was English in the hull and raking step of her masts, while the rigging, and the way in which she was managed, smacked so strongly of the Mediterranean that her nation also might have puzzled one familiar with such a subject. The lofty spread of canvas, the jib, flying-jib and fore-staysail, that are rarely worn save by the larger class of merchantmen, gave rather an odd appearance to a craft that could count hardly more than an hundred tons measurement.

Besides her fore and mainsail, and those already named, the schooner, for so we must call her, carried two heavy, but graceful topsails upon her fore and mainmasts, and even a jigger sail or spanker and gaff above it, on a slender spur rigged from the quarter deck. Altogether the schooner with her various appurtenances, resembled such a yacht as some of the English noblemen sail in the channel and about the Isle of Man in the sporting season.

The schooner was not unobserved from the shore, and a careful observer could have noticed a group of persons that were evidently regarding her with no common interest from the landing just above the harbor of Anapa.

"That must be the craft that has been so long expected," said one of the group, "and we had best get our girls ready at once to put on board before the morning."

"This comes in a bad time, for the steamer should be here before nightfall."

"That's true; as she doesn't seem inclined to run in too close, perhaps she knows it."

"What was the signal agreed upon?" asked the first speaker of his companion, who was silently regarding the schooner.

"A red flag at the foretopmast head, and there it goes. Yes, it is here sure enough."

"How like a witch she looks."

"They say she will outsail anything between here and Gibraltar, in any wind."

"What does that mean? she's going about."

"Sure enough, and up goes her foresail, they work with a will and are in a hurry."

"She don't like the looks of something on the coast," said the other.

The fact was, while the schooner lay under the easy sail we have described, just off the port of Anapa, the little Russian government steamer that plies between Odessa and the ports along the Circassian coast held by the emperor's troops, hove in sight, having just come down the Sea of Azoff through the Straits of Yorkcale. Her dark line of smoke was discovered by those on board the schooner, before she had doubled the headland of Tatman, and it was very plain, that, let the schooner's purpose be what it might, she desired to avoid all unnecessary observation, and especially that of the steamer.

A single movement of the helm while the mainsail sheet was eased away, and the schooner brought the gentle night breeze that was still setting from the north and east off the Georgian shore, right aft, and quietly hoisting her foresail, the two were set wing and wing, and a sea bird could not have skimmed with a more easy and graceful motion over the deep waters that glanced beneath her hull, than she did now. If the steamer had desired she might have overhauled the schooner, but it would have taken all night to do it with that leading wind in her favor; and so, after looking towards the clipper craft with her bows for a moment, the steamer again held on her course.

"Too swift of wing for that smoke pipe of yours," said one of the Circassians who had been watching the evolutions of the two crafts from the shore.

"The steamer has put her helm down and gives it up for it bad job," said another, as her black bow came once more to look towards the port of Anapa.

"She will be off before night sets in, and we shall have the schooner back again."

This was in fact the policy of those on board the schooner; for no sooner did she find herself unpursued than she hauled her wind, jibed her foresail to starboard and looked down, towards the coast of Asia Minor, until the moon crept up from behind the mountains of the Caucasus as though it had come from a bath in the Caspian Sea beyond, when the schooner was closer hauled on the other trick, and bore up again for the harbor of Anapa.

We have said that the little clipper numbered some hundred tons, but though her appearance would indicate this to be the case, yet your thorough-bred sailor would have marked how stiffly she bore so much top hamper, and would have judged more correctly by the depth of water that the schooner evidently drew. It was plain that she was deep and much heavier than she looked. A few sprightly Greek youths, in their picturesque costume were dispersed here and there in the waist and on the forecastle, while two or three persons wearing the same dress and evidently of that nation, were talking together in a group upon the weather-side of the quarter-deck.

As the hours drew towards midnight, the schooner at length opened communication with the land by means of signal lanterns, and immediately after boats commenced to ply between the clipper and the shore, and continued to do so for several hours. It was plain enough to any one who knew the usages and trade of these waters, that the schooner was preparing to run a cargo of Circassian girls, the trade having been, as we have already shown, made contraband by the Russians.

At last the clipper seemed to have received all on board that she expected in the shape of passengers, but still stood off and on for some reason until the breaking day began to tinge the mountain tops beyond Anapa; when a last boat with five persons, one of whom was a female, came down to the clipper which was thrown in the wind's eye long enough for those to get on board, or rather for three of them to do so; and then, as the other two pulled back to the shore, the schooner gradually came round under the force of her topsail, and one sail after another was distended and sheeted home until she looked to those on shore as though enveloped in canvas, and drove over the waters like a flying cloud.

One of those who pulled away from the schooner as she lay her course, would have been recognized by the reader as Krometz; and now half way to the landing he motioned his companion to cease rowing, while he paused himself and looked after the receding clipper with a strange medley of expression pictured in his face.

"Give way, give way," said his companion at last, somewhat impatiently; "one would think, by the way you look seaward, that you would like to head in that direction instead of pulling into the harbor."

"You are right, comrade. I do wish that yonder clipper was carrying me away from here."

"You are a queer fellow, Krometz, to let that girl make you so unhappy, but she's off now, and will probably bring up in some Turkish harem, where she will end her days. Not so bad a fate either," continued the oarsman. "Surrounded by every luxury the heart could wish or the imagination conceive, it's a better lot than either yours or mine."

"Well, say no more of this, and remember the utmost secrecy is to be observed, for that tiger of an Aphiz will hunt us to death if he does but suspect that we had a hand in the business."

"Our disguise was sufficient," said the other, "and by-the-way, we may as well get rid of this black stuff now;" and as he spoke he dashed the water from alongside upon his face and hands, and removed a coat of black from them.

"Now give way again; let us get in, and separate before any one is stirring abroad."

Leaving Krometz and his companion to pursue their own business, and the clipper craft with her course laid for the Sea of Marmora, we will, with the reader, return once more to the mountain side where we met Komel and Aphiz.

In time of peace, or rather when there was no open outbreak between the Circassians and the Russian forces, Aphiz Adegah passed his time in hunting among the rugged hills and cliffs, and with the early morn was abroad with his gun strapped to his back, and in his hand the long iron-pointed staff that helped him to climb the otherwise inaccessible rocks of the mountain's sides. Thus equipped, he came, in the morning referred to above, to the cottage of Komel's parents, but, instead of the cheerful, happy welcome that usually greeted him on such occasions, he beheld consternation and misery written in the father's face, while the mother wept as though her heart would break.

"What means this strange scene?" asked the young hunter, hastily. "Where is Komel?"

"Alas! gone, gone," sighed both.

"Gone!"

"Ay, gone forever."

"What mean you? whither has she gone? what has happened to render you so miserable?"

Alas, Aphiz; Komel has gone to be the star of some proud Turkish harem," said the father.

"And with your consent?"

"No! O, no!"

"Nor by her own free will, that I know," he continued, quickly.

"Alas! no; this night she was stolen from us, and we saw her borne away before our very eyes."

"Was there no one by to strike a blow for her, no one to render you aid?"

"Yes, one there was, an honest friend who lives in the next cottage. He was aroused by the noise, and outraged by the violence he beheld, he rushed upon the thieves, but they struck him bleeding and dead to the earth. It was a terrible sight and poor Komel saw it as they carried her away, and uttered such a fearful, piercing scream that it seems to ring in our cars even now. She fainted then in their arms, and we saw her no more."

"Heaven guard her!" said Aphiz, with inward anguish expressed in his face.

"Amen!" said the aged father, with a deep, heartfelt sigh, full of sorrow.

This told the whole story of the previous night, and the last boat that put off from, the shore for the clipper schooner contained Komel as a prisoner, insensible to all about, abducted by her own countrymen, incited by the revengeful spirit of Krometz. Actuated by the vilest motives himself, he had persuaded a companion, as we have seen, by a small bribe and the representation that Komel would in reality be better off than with her parents, to aid him in his object. Krometz had not hesitated to receive the handsome sum that one so beautiful as Komel could not fail to command.

Aphiz was almost too miserable to be able to find words to express his feelings. A bitter tear stole down his sunburnt check as he saw the mother's grief, but a stern flash of the eye was also visible in the expression of his face. He sought at once the highest cliff beyond the cottage, and in the distant, far-off horizon, could dimly make out the white canvas of the slave cutter, no bigger than a sea-bird, on the skirts of the horizon. He sat down in the bitterness of his anguish, alone and heart-broken, and then he remembered the scene of the previous evening, how they both together had seen the hawk pounce down and carry off in its talons the poor wood dove.

That scene, so suggestive to his mind, was not without its meaning. It was the forerunner of the calamity under which his heart now grieved so bitterly. Aphiz Adegah's life had been a bold one, he knew no fear. The air of his native hills was not freer than his own spirit and as he looked off once more at the tiny white speck in the distance that marked the spot where Komel was, his resolution was instantly made, and he swore to follow and rescue her.

It was but natural that the young mountaineer should desire to find out the agency by which that evil business had been consummated. He knew very well that such a plan as Komel's abduction could not have been perpetrated without the aid of parties that knew her and her home, but never for one moment did he suspect Krometz. He had ever professed the warmest friendship for both him and Komel, and he was deemed honest. But during the melee, when the honest mountaineer had rushed to Komel's rescue, and had received the fatal blow, her parents heard a voice that they recognized, and both exclaimed, "Can that voice be Krometz's!"

This was afterwards made known to Aphiz, and with this clue, though he could scarcely believe that there was the possibility of fact or correctness in the surmise, he sought his pretended friend. He charged him with the evidence and its inference, and bade him speak and say if this was true.

"It matters not, friend Aphiz, since she is gone, how she came to go."

"This answer," said the young mountaineer, "is but another evidence against thee."

"Do you pretend to call me to an account, Aphiz? You are but a boy, while I have already reached the full age of manhood. Think not, because you were more successful with that girl, than I, that you can lord it over me. I shall answer no further charges from you."

"Krometz, your guilt speaks out in every line of your face," said the excited Aphiz. "Meet me at sunset behind the signal rock on the cliff, and we will settle this affair together."

"I will neither meet thee, nor account to thee for aught I may have done."

"The, as true as to-morrow's sun shall rise, with this good rifle I will shoot you to the heart. I shall be there at the sunset hour; fail me, and to-morrow you shall die."

Krometz knew well with whom he had to deal; he knew if he met Aphiz, as he proposed, there would be a chance for his life, but if he failed him, he feared the unerring aim of his rifle. He was no coward — both of them had faced the enemy together, but he lacked the moral courage that is far more sustaining than mere dogged bravery, or contempt for immediate danger. Thus influence, at sunset he kept the appointment.

The young mountaineer had been taught this mode of resort to arms by the Russian and Polish officers who had been thrown much among them. They had no seconds, but fought alone, starting back to back, walking forward five paces, wheeling and firing together. The position was on the brink of a precipice, and he who fell would be hurled at once down an immense depth. Aphiz was desperate, Krometz reckless; they fired and the body of the latter fell over the cliff. Aphiz was unharmed.

In a moment after he realized his situation, has act, however just, had made him a fugitive, and he must fly at once from those scenes of his boyish love and happiness.

CHAPTER VI.

A SINGULAR MEETING.

Turning from the mountain scenes we have described, let us back once more to Constantinople, and direct our footsteps up the fragrant valley where the Barbyses threads its meandering course. Here let us look once more into the gilded cage that holds the Sultan's favorites, where art had exhausted itself to form a fairy-like spot, as beautiful as the imagination could conceive. We find here, once more, amid the fragrant atmosphere and the playing fountains, the form of Lalla, and by her side again that form, before which all the tribes of the faithful kneel in humble submission. It was strange what a potent charm the dumb but beautiful Circassian had thrown about herself. It seemed as though some fairy circle enshrined her, within which no harm might possibly reach the gentle slave.

An observant person could have noticed also a third party in that presence, though he was some distance from Lalla's side, lying upon the ground, so near the jet of a fountain, that the spray dampened his face. It was the idiot. To the monarch, or his slave, he appeared unconscious of aught save the play of water; but one nearer to him would have seen that no movement of either escaped the now watchful eye of the boy. Was it possible that he possessed a degree of reason, after all, and more than half assumed the strange guise that seemed to enshroud his wits.

Now he tossed the pure white pebble stones into the playing waters, and saw them carried up by the force of the jets, and now half rising to his elbow, startled the gold and silver fish in the basin by a tiny shower of gravel, but still with a strange tenacity, ever watching both the Sultan and his slave, though not appearing to do so.

A change had come over that proud, eastern prince. He had been awakened to fresh impulses, and a new and joyful sense of realization; the sentiments that actuated him were novel, indeed, to his breast. From childhood he had been taught by every association to look upon the gentler sex as toys, merely, of his own; but here was one, yes, and the first one, too, who had caused him to realize that she had a soul, a heart, a brilliant, natural intelligence of mind, that surprised and delighted him. Besides this, the fact of her sad physical misfortune had, no doubt, increased his tender and respectful solicitude, and thus altogether he was most peculiarly situated, as it regarded his dumb slave.

The stern warrior, the relentless foe, the severe judge, and the pampered monarch, all were merged in the man, when by her side—and Sultan Mahomet, for the first time in his life, felt that he loved!

As we have shown, it was not the headstrong promptings of passion that actuated him—far from it; for had the monarch been heedless of her love and respect in return, how easily might he have commanded any submission, on her part, that he could wish. The truth was, he feared to risk the love he now felt that he coveted so strongly, by any overt act, and thus day by day her life stole quietly on, and lie was still ever tender and respectful, ever thoughtful for her comfort or pleasure, and ever assiduous to make her feel contented and happy with her lot.

It would have been most unnatural had not Lalla experienced, in return for all this kindness, the warmest sentiments of gratitude, and this she showed in the expression of her dark, dreamy eyes, at all times; and to speak truly, the Sultan felt himself amply repaid by her gentle gratitude and tender smiles.

In the mean time, as days and weeks passed on, silently registering the course of life, the chill of homesickness, which had been so keen and saddening at first, wore gradually away from the radiant face of the slave, though she thought no less earnestly and dearly of her friends and her home, far away in the Circassian hills; yet absence and time had robbed her grief of its keenness, while the easy and luxuriant mode of living that she enjoyed had again restored the roundness of her beautiful form, had once more imparted the rose to her check, and the elasticity of her childhood's day to her movements. In short, she who was so lovely when she entered the harem, had now grown so much more so, that the companions who surrounded her, with sentiments almost akin to awe, declared her too beautiful to live, and sagely hinting that ere long she would hear the songs of those spirits who chant around Allah's throne.

All this had wrought a corresponding change in the heart of the Sultan; indeed his affection and, interest for Lalla had even more than kept pace with this improvement in her appearance; and now it was for the first time since she came there, that those scarcely less beautiful Georgians, the petted favorites, heretofore, of the monarch, now evinced feelings of envy that it was impossible to disguise. They saw but too plainly that the Sultan cared only for the dumb slave, had smiles for no one else, and that he was ever by her side when within the precincts of the harem.

Nor is it to be wondered at that they should feel thus. In a country where personal beauty constitutes the marketable value of a woman, it was but natural, that they should be led to prize this endowment, and perhaps also in the end to dislike all who should successfully contest the palm with them in this respect. Still, so sweet was Lalla's disposition, so yielding and considerate, that they could not openly express the feelings that brooded in their breasts; nor had one unkind word yet been expressed towards her, since the first hour that she had entered the Sultan's household.

Leaving the dumb slave thus bound by silken cords, thus chained in a gilded cage, we will once more turn to the fortunes of the lone and weary traveller, whom we left in the Armenian quarter of the capital.

He was evidently a wanderer, and, save the liberal means he had received from the hands of the grateful Turk whom he had so providentially rescued near the forest borders of Belgrade, he was poor indeed. Yet with strict economy this purse had served him well, and for a long while; whatever his errand in this capital might be, he seemed to keep it sacredly to himself, and to wander day after day, front morning until night, here, there, and everywhere, now in the slave market, now in the opium bazaar, now among the silk merchants, now among the splendid and picturesque dwellings along the banks of the Bosphorus, and now in this quarter, now in that, seemingly in search of some one he hoped to find; but as night returned, he, too, came to his temporary home, tired, dejected and unhappy.

But day after day and week after week had at last entirely emptied his purse of its golden contents, and he stood now very near the spot where we first introduced him to the reader. The purse was in his hand, and he was consulting with himself now as to what course he should pursue for the future, when his eyes rested once more upon the jewelled receptacle he held in his hand. He had often marked its richness, and the thought came across him that he might realize a small sum by selling it at some of the fancy bazaars, and he had even made up his mind to adopt this plan, when he suddenly remembered, for the first time, that the Turk had told him to present it at the gates of the seraglio gardens when he needed further aid.

"Fool that I have been!" ejaculated the wanderer, vehemently, "perhaps I might not only obtain the necessary pecuniary aid from him, but also that information which I so sadly but earnestly seek. Why should I, until this late hour, have forgotten his proffered aid? I will away to him at once, tell him my sad history, and beseech him to lend me the assistance I require." Thus saying, he turned his eyes towards the little point of land that jets out towards Asia from the Turkish city, known as Seraglio Point, a fairy-like cluster of gardens and palaces marking the spot.

His quick, nervous step soon brought him to the gilded portal that formed the entrance to the splendid gardens beyond, and through the sentinel who guarded the spot he summoned an officer of the household, to whom he showed the purse, telling him that he had received it from the owner as a token of friendship, and that he had bidden him, when necessity should dictate, to show it at the seraglio gates, and he would be admitted to his presence.

"God is great!" said the officer, as he looked upon the purse with a profound reverence, astonishing the humble wanderer by the respect he showed to the jewelled bag.

"And what place is this?" he asked of the officer, as hie looked curiously about him.

"By the beard of the Prophet, young man, do you not know?" asked the official.

"I do not."

"Not know whose purse you hold, and in whose grounds you stand!" reiterated the soldier.

"Not I."

"Allah akbar! it is the palace of the defender of the faith, Sultan Mahomet!"

"The Sultan!" exclaimed the lone wanderer, struck dumb with amazement.

"The Brother of the Sun," repeated the official, with a profound salaam as he repeated the name, while at the same time he noted the astonishment of the stranger.

"The Sultan," repeated the new comer, musing to himself, "rides he forth alone?"

"At times, yes, when it suits him. No harm can come to him—he is sacred, and need not fear."

"Perhaps not," answered the other, as he recalled the scene on the borders of the forest.

At the singular piece of intelligence which the had received, the stranger seemed to hesitate. He surely would not have come hither had he known to whom he was about to apply for assistance. Could it be the Sultan that he so opportunely aided? If so, he surely need not fear to meet him again; perhaps he might even venture still to tell him honestly his story, and ask at least for advice in the pursuit of the object which had brought him to Constantinople. In this half undecided mood he stood musing for some minutes, and then with a struggle for resolution, bade the officer lead him to his master.

Let us look in upon the royal presence for a moment. It is a gorgeous saloon, where the monarch lounges upon satin cushions, with the rich amber mouthpiece of his pipe between his lips, and the perfumed tobacco gently wreathing in blue smoke above his head. Mahomet was at this moment seated on a pedestal of cushions, so rich and soft that he seemed almost, lost in their luxuriance. Reclining by his side was a creature so lovely in her maidenly beauty, that pencil, not pen, should describe her. Ever and anon the monarch cast glances of such tenderness towards her that an unprejudiced observer would have noticed at once the warmth of his feelings towards her, while the gentle slave, for it was Lalla, turned over a pile of rich English engravings, pausing now and then to hold one of more than usual interest before his eyes.

It was an interesting scene. The pictures had deeply interested the slave, and with graceful abandon she had forgotten everything but them; now smiling over some curious representation, or sighing over another no less truthful, and her fair, young face expressing the feelings that actuated her bosom with telltale accuracy all the while. Her dark hair was interwoven with pearls by the running hands of the Nubian slaves, and its long plaits reached nearly to her feet, while across her fair brow there hung a cluster of diamonds which might have ransomed an emperor—a gift from the Sultan himself.

The Sultan seemed, of late, scarcely contented to have her from his side for a single hour, and even received his officials and gave audience, with her in the presence oftentimes, first motioning her, on such occasions, to cover her face, after the style of the Turkish women; but even this precaution was rarely taken, for Lalla was not used to it, and the Sultan pressed nothing upon her that he found to be in any way disagreeable to her feelings. So when the officer announced a stranger who had shown a purse which bore the Sultan's arms as his talisman, he was bidden to admit him at once.

The slave turned her back by chance as the stranger entered, and hearing not his steps she still bent absorbedly over the roll of engravings while the new comer with profound respect told the Sultan that until a moment since he had not known that it was his good fortune to have served his highness, and that perhaps had he realized this he would not then be before him.—But the monarch generously re-assured him by his kindness, and repeated his offer of any service in his power.

"I feel that I am already a heavy pensioner on your bounty, excellency," he replied.

"Not so; your bravery and prompt assistance stood us in aid at an important moment.—Speak then, and if there be aught in which we can further your wishes or good, it will afford us pleasure."

"It is of a matter, which would hardly interest your excellency that I would speak."

"We are the best judge of that matter."

"Shall I tell my story then, excellency?"

"Ay, speak on," said the monarch, resuming his pipe, and pouring forth a lazy cloud of smoke from his mouth.

"Excellency," he commenced, "I am it very humble mountaineer of the Caucasus, but until these few months past have been as happy as heart could wish. True, we have often been called upon to confront the Cossack, but that is a duty and a pleasure, and the tide of battle once over, we have returned with renewed joy to our cottage homes. Our hearths are rude and homely, but our wants are few, and our hearts are warm among our native hills.

"Suddenly, a hawk swooped down upon our mountain side, and bore away the sweetest and most innocent dove that nestled there, making desolate many hearts, and causing an aged mother and father to weep tears of bitter anguish. I loved that being, excellency, so well that my whole soul was hers, and she too in turn loved me. Broken hearted and most miserable I have wandered hither to seek her, for hither I found that she had been brought, and perhaps even now is the unhappy slave of some heartless one, and is pining for the home she has been torn from. If you would bless me, excellency, ay, bless yourself by a noble deed, then aid me to find her in this great capital."

The monarch listened with unfeigned interest, he, had a strong dash of romance in his disposition, besides which he could feel for the disconsolate lover now, since his own heart bad been so awakened to itself.

"Your story interests me," said the Sultan, still regarding him intently.

"It is very simple, excellency, but alas! it is also very true," was the reply.

"What name do you bear?"

"Aphiz Adegah, excellency!"

"And what was her name of whom you have spoken?"

"Her name was Komel."

At the same moment that he answered thus, Lalla turned by chance from her engravings, towards them, when her eyes resting upon those of Aphiz, she rose, staggered a few steps towards him, and uttered a scream so shrill and piercing that even the imperturbable Turk sprang to his feet in amazement, while Aphiz cried:

"It is she, it is my lost Komel!"

47

CHAPTER VII.

THE SULTAN'S PRISONER.

The Sultan was as capable of revenge as he was of love or gratitude, and this, Aphiz was destined to learn to his sorrow; for no sooner did the monarch comprehend the scene we have just described, after having heard the story of Aphiz related, than he immediately summoned the guard, and the young Circassian found himself borne away to a place of confinement within the seraglio gardens, where he was left alone to ponder upon his singular situation. It was not an easy task for him to divest his mind of the thought that all was a dream, so singular were the threads of the past woven together since the happy hours when Komel and himself bade good night at her father's cottage door.

As to the fair and beautiful slave herself, she was conducted back to the harem, at the same time that Aphiz was borne away to prison, but a new world had opened to her. Her voice and hearing, lost by the fearful shock she had realized by that sight of bloodshed on the night when they stole her away from her parents, had, strangely enough, been again restored by a shock scarcely less potent in its effect upon her. That startling scream which she uttered on beholding Aphiz had loosened the portals of her ears, and the violent effort made in order to utter that exclamation had again loosened the power of utterance. In spite of the attending circumstances, she could not but rejoice at the return of those faculties that she had now been taught the value of.

The delight of the Sultan at Komel's recovery of her speech and hearing, was only equalled by his uneasiness at the extraordinary position of affairs between himself and the man who had so gallantly saved his life on the Belgrade plains. Loving his slave so tenderly, what could he do under the circumstances? He now found the music of her voice as delicious as the almost angelic beauty of her form and features, and so charmed was he with the improvement that Komel evinced, and so did he love to listen to her voice, that he could even bear to hear her plead for Aphiz, and beseech that he might be brought to her. Much as this would have been against his own feelings and wishes, still to have her talk to him he listened patiently, or seemed to do so, even while she besought him thus.

There was another being whose joy at Komel's recovery of her speech seemed, if possible, more extravagant even than the Sultan's, and far more remarkable in manifestation. When the idiot boy first heard her voice, he started, and crouching like an animal, crept away to a spot whence he could observe her without himself being seen. By degrees he drew nearer, and finally received her kind tokens without any evidences of fear. And by degrees, as she spoke to him and tutored her words to his simple capacity, he seemed to be filled with the very ecstasy of joy, and ran and leaped like a hound newly loosed from confinement. Then he would return, and taking her hand, place it upon his forehead and temples, and then curling his body into a ball, lie motionless by her side.

"You love this young Circassian, and would leave me and your present home for him?" asked the Sultan, as Komel entered the reception saloon in answer to a summons he had sent to her.

"I do love him, excellency," replied the slave, honestly; "we were children together, and I cannot remember the time when I loved him not, for we were always as brother and sister."

"There are not many of thy nation, Komel, who would choose an humble mountaineer to a Sultan," said the monarch, with a bitter intonation of voice.

"Alas! excellency," she replied, "too many of my untutored countrywomen, being brought up from their infancy to consider it as their infallible lot, make a barter of their hearts for gold. Such know no true promptings of love."

"You are happy and contented here, you want for nothing, you are the mistress of this broad palace. Bid me send thy countryman away loaded with gold, and we will live always together."

"Excellency, I am not happy here, and though I participate in all the splendor you so liberally furnish for me, my heart, alas! is ever straying back to my humble home."

"This feeling of discontent will soon die away, Komel, and you will be happy again," said the Sultan, toying with her delicate hands which had been tipped at the finger ends by the Nubian slaves with the henna dye.

"Never, excellency, my early home and my heart will always be together," she replied, with a sigh.

"Nevertheless, Komel," continued the Sultan in a decided tone of voice, "you are my slave, and I love you. This being the case, think you I shall be very ready to part with you?"

"Ah! excellency, you are too generous, too kind-hearted, to detain me here against my wishes. I know this by the gentle and considerate care I have already received at your hands."

"You mistake, you mistake," repeated the Sultan, earnestly; "that was because I loved you so well, Komel. I saw in you, not only the transparent beauty with which Heaven has endowed your race, but a soul and intelligence that won my heart. Your infirmity, now so suddenly removed, demanded for you every consideration, but now aroused by the opposition that circumstances seem to have woven around me, other feelings are fast becoming rooted in my breast. Shall such as I am be thwarted in my wish by an humble mountaineer of the Caucasus?"

As the monarch spoke thus he laid aside the mouth-piece of his pipe, and leaning upon his elbow amid the yielding cushions, covered his face with his hand and seemed lost in silent meditation.

The beautiful slave regarded him intently while he remained in this position. His uniform kindness to her for so long a period had led her to regard him with no slight attachment, but she knew that Aphiz was at that very moment under close confinement within the palace walls for his faithfulness in following and seeking her, and as she was wholly his before, this but endeared him more earnestly to her. All the splendor that Sultan Mahomet could offer her, the rank and wealth, were all counted as naught in comparison with the tender affection which had grown up with her from childhood.

She awaited in silence the monarch's mood, but resolved to appeal to his mercy, and beg him to release both Aphiz and herself, that they might return together once more to their distant home.

But alas! how utterly useless were all her efforts to this end. They were received by the Sultan in that cold, irascible spirit that seems to form so large a share of the Turkish character. Her words seemed only to arouse and fret him now, and she could see in his looks of fixed determination and resolve that in the end he would stop at no means to gratify his own wishes, and that perhaps, Aphiz's life alone would satisfy his bitter spirit. It was a fearful thought that he should be sacrificed for her sake, and she trembled as she looked into the dark depths of his stern, cold eye, which had never beamed on her thus before.

She crept nearer to his side, and raising his hand within her own, besought him to look kindly upon her again, to smile on her as he used to do. It was a gentle, confiding and entreating appeal, and for a moment the stern features of the monarch did relent, but it was for an instant only his thoughts troubled him, and he was ill at ease.

In the meantime Aphiz Adegah found himself confined in a close prison; the entire current of his feelings were changed by the discovery he had made. Not having been able to exchange one word with Komel, of course he could not possibly know aught of her real situation further than appearances indicated by her presence there, and he could not but tremble at the fear that naturally suggested itself to his mind as to the relationship which she bore to the Sultan—In this painful state of doubt, he counted the weary hours in his lonely cell, and calmly awaited his impending fate, let it be what it might.

He knew the summary mode in which Turkish justice was administered; he was not unfamiliar with the dark stories that were told of sunken bodies about the outer bastion of the palace where its walls were laved by the Bosphorus. He knew very well that an unfaithful wife or rival lover was often sacrificed to the pride or revenge of any titled or rich Turk who happened to possess the power to enable him to carry out his purpose. Knowing all this he prepared his mind for whatever might come, and had he been summoned to follow a guard detailed to sink him in the sea, he would not have been surprised. The idiot boy, half-witted as he was, seemed at once by some natural instinct to divine the relationship that existed between Komel and the prisoner, and suggested to her a plan of communication with him by means of flowers. She saw the boy gather up a handful of loose buds and blossoms from her lap several times, and observed him carry them away. Curiosity led her to see what he did with then, and she followed him as far as she might do consistently with the rules of the harem, and from thence observed him scale a tree that overhung a dark sombre-looking building, and toss the flowers through a small window, into what she knew at once must be Aphiz's cell.

In childhood, Aphiz and herself had often interpreted to each other the language of flowers, and now hastening back to the luxuriant conservatory of plants, she culled such as she desired, and arranging them with nervous fingers, told in their fragrant folds how tenderly she still loved him, and that she was still true to their plighted faith.

Entrusting this to the boy she indicated what he was to do with it, while the poor half-witted being seemed in an ecstacy of delight at his commission, and soon deposited the precious token inside the window of Aphiz's prison.

It needed no conjuror to tell Aphiz whom that floral letter came from. The shower of buds and blossoms that had been thrown to him by the boy had puzzled him, coming without any apparent design, regularity, or purpose; but this, as he read its hidden mystery, was all clear enough to him, he knew the hand that had to gathered and bound them together. She was true and loved him still.

Komel, in her earnest love, despite the rebuff she had already received, determined once more to appeal to the Sultan for the release of his prisoner. But the monarch had grown moody and thoughtful, as we have seen, when he realized that his slave loved another; and every word she now uttered in his behalf was bitterness to his very soul. She only found that he was the more firmly set in his design as to retraining her in the harem, if not to take the life of the young mountaineer.

The Sultan brooded over this state of affairs with a settled frown upon his brow. Had it not been that Aphiz had saved his life by his brave assistance at a critical moment, he would not have hesitated one instant as to what he should do, for had it been otherwise he would have ordered him to be destroyed as quickly as he would have ordered the execution of any criminal.—But hardened and calloused as he was by power, and self-willed as he was from never being thwarted in his wishes, yet he found it difficult to give the order that should sacrifice the life of one who had so gallantly saved him from peril.

At last the monarch seemed to have resolved upon some plan, whereby he hoped to relieve himself from the dilemma that so seriously annoyed him. He was most expert at disguises; indeed, it was often his custom to walk the streets of his capital incog, or to ride out unattended, in a plain citizen's dress, as we have seen, that he might the better observe for himself those things concerning which he required accurate information. It was then nothing new for him to don the dress of an officer of the household guard; and in this costume he visited Aphiz in his cell, representing himself to be the agent of the Sultan.

"I come as an agent of the Sultan," he said, as the turnkey introduced him to the cell.

"The Sultan is very gracious to remember' me; what is his will?" asked the prisoner.

"He has a proposition to offer you, to which, if you accede, you are at once free to go from here."

"And what are these terms?" asked Aphiz, with perfect coolness.

"That you instantly leave Constantinople, never again to return to it."

"Alone?"

"Except that he will fill a purse with gold for thee to help thee on thy homeward way."

"I shall never leave the city alone," replied the prisoner, with firmness.

"Is that your answer?"

"As well thus perhaps as any way. I shall never leave this city without Komel."

"But if you remain it may cost you your life," continued the stranger.

"I do not fear death," replied the Circassian, with the utmost coolness.

"A painful and degrading death," suggested the agent, earnestly.

"I care not. I have faced death in too many forms to fear him in any."

"Stubborn man!" continued the visiter, irritated in the extreme at the cool decision and dauntless bravery of the prisoner, adding, "you tempt your own fate by refusing this generous offer."

"No fate can be worse than to be separated from her I love. If that is to be done, then welcome death; for life without her would cease to be desirable."

"Do not be hasty in your decision."

"I am all calmness," was the reply.

"And shall I bear your refusal to leave the city, to the Sultan? Weigh the matter well; you can return to your native land with a purse heavy with gold, but if you remain you die."

"You have then my plain refusal of the terms. Tell the Sultan for me," —Aphiz in his acuteness easily penetrated the monarch's disguise, — "tell him I thank him heartily for the generous means that he afforded me when I was poor and needy, and whereby I have been supported in his capital so long. Tell him too that I forgive him for this causeless imprisonment, and that if it be his will that I should die, because I love one who has loved me from childhood, I forgive him that also."

"You will not reconsider this answer."

"I am firm, and no casualty can alter my feelings, no threats can alarm me."

The visiter could not suppress his impatience at these remarks, but telling Aphiz that if he repeated his answer to the Sultan he feared that it would seal his fate forever, he left him once more alone.

Aphiz, as we have said, knew very well who had visited him in his cell, and now that he was gone he composed himself as best he could, placing Komel's bouquet in his bosom and trying to sleep, for it was now night. But he felt satisfied in his own mind that his worst expectations would be realized ere long, for he had marked well the expression of the Sultan's face, and he fell asleep to dream that he had bidden Komel and life itself adieu.

And while he, whom she loved so well, lay upon the damp floor of the cell to sleep, Komel lounged on a couch of downy softness, and was lulled to sleep by the playing of sweet fountains, and the gentle notes of the lute played by a slave, close by her couch, that her dreams might be sweet and her senses beguiled to rest by sweet harmony. But the lovely girl forgot him not, and her dreams were of him as her waking thoughts were ever full of him.

What is there, this side of heaven, brighter than the enduring constancy of woman?

CHAPTER VIII.

PUNISHMENT OF THE SACK.

The sun was almost set, and the soft twilight was creeping over the incomparable scenery that renders the coast of Marmora so beautiful; the gilded spires of the oriental capital were not more brilliant than the dimpled surface of the sea where it opened and spread away from the mouth of the Bosphorus. The blue waters had robbed the evening sky of its blushing tints, and seemed to revel in the richness of its coloring.—It was at this calm and quiet hour that a caique, propelled by a dozen oarsmen, shot out from the shore of the Seraglio Point, and swept round at once with its prow turned towards the open sea. In the stern at two dark, uncouth looking Turks, between whom was a young man who seemed to be under restraint, and in whom the reader would have recognized Aphiz, the Sultan's prisoner.

It was plain that the caique was bound on some errand of more than ordinary interest, and many eyes from the shore were regarding it curiously, as did also the various boat crews that met it on the water.

Still it held on its way steadily, propelled by the long, regular stroke of the oarsmen over the half mile of blue water that separates Europe and Asia at this point, sweeping as it went by, lovely villages, mosques, minarets, and the dark cemeteries that line the shores, until, a certain point having been gained, the oarsmen at a signal from those in the stern, rested from their labors, while the boat still glided on from the impetus it had received. In a moment more, Aphiz was completely covered with a large, stout canvas bag or sack, which was secured about him and tied up. At one extremity was attached a heavy shot, and when these preparations were completed, he was cast into the sea, sinking as quickly from sight as a stone might have done. A few bubbles rose to the surface where the sack had gone down, and all was over. The bows of the caique were instantly turned towards the city, and the men gave way as carelessly as though nothing uncommon had transpired.

Aphiz had thus been made to suffer the penalty usually inflicted upon certain crimes, and especially to the wives of such of the Turks as suspected them of inconstancy, a punishment that is even to this day common in Constantinople. The Sultan had reasoned that if Komel knew Aphiz Adegah to be dead, she would after awhile recover from the shock, and gradually forgetting him, receive his own regard instead of that of the young mountaineer, as he would have her do voluntarily; for he felt, as much as he coveted her favor, that he could never claim her for a wife unless it was with her own consent and free will. If he had not love her, he would have felt differently, and would have commanded that favor which now would lose its charms unless 'twas wooed and won.

But we shall see how mistaken the monarch was in his selfish calculations.

Reasoning upon the grounds that we have named, the Sultan had ordered Aphiz to be drowned in the Bosphorus, as we have seen, and the deed was performed by the regular executioners of government. The Sultan was supreme, and his orders were obeyed without question; this being the case, Aphiz's fate caused no remark even among the gossips.

The few days that had transpired since Komel had regained her speech and hearing, had of course taught her more in relation to her actual situation and the character of those about her than she had been able to gather by silent observation during her entire previous confinement in the harem of the palace.

She was aware that the Sultan was impetuous and self-willed, but she could hardly bring her mind to believe that he would actually put in practice such a piece of villany as should cost Aphiz his life. Knowing as much as she did of his imperious and stern habits, she did not believe him capable of such cold-blooded baseness. But no sooner had the officers, sent to execute his sentence against the innocent mountaineer, returned and announced the task as performed, than Komel was summoned to the presence of the the Sultan.

"I have sent for you, Komel," said the monarch, while he regarded her intently as he spoke, "to tell you that Aphiz is dead."

"Dead, excellency; do you say dead?"

"Yes."

"You do but jest with me, excellency," she said, trying in her tremor to smile.

"I rarely jest with any one and surely should not have sent for you were I in that mood. He has gone to make food for the fishes at the bottom of the Bosphorus."

"Has his life been taken by your orders, excellency?" she asked, with a pallid cheek and blanched lips.

"You have said," answered the Sultan.

"Ah! excellency, I am but a weak girl and can ill abide a jest. Aphiz can have done nothing to receive your displeasure, and surely you would not take his life without reason."

"I had reason sufficient for me."

"What was it, excellency?"

"The fellow loved you, Komel."

"O, sorrow me, sorrow me, that his love for should have been his ending."

The struggle in the beautiful girl's bosom for a moment was fearful. It was like the rough and sudden blast that sweeps tempest—like over a glassy lake and turns its calm waters into trembling waves and dark shadows. She did not give way under the fearful news that she hear; a counter current of feeling seemed to save her, and to bring back the color once more to her lips, and cheeks, and to add brilliancy to the large, lustrous eyes so peculiar to her race. All this the Sultan marked well, and indeed was at a loss rightly to understand these demonstrations.

So quick and marked was the change that it puzzled the monarch, though he read something still of its rightful character, for he had known before the bitterness of a revengeful spirit, and bore upon his breast, at that hour, the deep impression of a dagger's point, where a Circassian slave, whom he had deprived of her child, had attempted to stab him to the heart. And now as he looked upon Komel, he thought he could read some such spirit in the expression of the beautiful slave before him, and he was right! Dark thoughts seemed to be struggling even in her gentle breast, when she realized that Aphiz was no more, and that his murderer was before her.

Nothing in reality could be more gentle than the loving disposition of the slave. Her natural character was all tenderness and modest diffidence, but she had now been touched at a point where she was most sensitive. Aphiz, without the shadow of guilt, save that he was true in his love to her, had been murdered in cold blood, and the announcement of the fact by the Sultan had chilled every fountain of tenderness in her bosom. She looked wistfully at the jewelled dagger that hung in the monarch's girdle, and fearful thoughts were thronging her brain. The Sultan little knew on how slender thread his life hung at that moment, for a very slight blow from his dagger, swiftly and truly given, would have revenged Aphiz in a moment.

"And what end do you propose to yourself that this deed has been done?" she asked, after a few moments' pause, during which the Sultan had regarded her most intently, and, if possible, with increased interest, at the picture she now presented of startled and spirited energy.

"You told me, Komel, that you loved him, did you not?" he asked.

"I did."

"Can you see no reason now why he should not live, at least, in Constantinople?"

"None."

"He had his choice, and was told that he might leave here in peace; but he chose to stay and die."

"And for his devotion to me you have killed him?" continued Komel, bitterly.

"Not for his devotion, but his stubbornness," said the Sultan. "Come, Komel, smile once more. He is dead-time flies quickly on, and he will soon be forgotten."

"Never!" replied the slave, with startling energy. "You will find that a Circassian's heart is not so easily moulded in a Turkish shape!"

The monarch bit his lip at the sarcasm of the remark, and as it, was expressed with no lack of bitterness, it could not but cut him keenly. Still preserving that calm self-possession which a full consciousness of his power imparted, he smiled instead of frowning upon her, and said:

"You are heated now; to-morrow, or perhaps the next day, you may come to me, and I trust that you will then be in a better humor than at present."

Komel bowed coldly at the intimation, while her expression told how bitterly she felt towards him.

A dark frown came over the Sultan's face at the same moment, and an accurate reader of physiognomy would have detected the fear expressed there that his violent purpose, as executed upon Aphiz, had failed totally of success.

Turning coldly away from him, the slave sought her own apartment in the gorgeous palace, to mourn in silence and alone over the fearful and bitter news she had just heard concerning one who was to her all in all, and who had taken with him her heart to the spirit land. The world, and all future time, looked to her like a blank, as though overspread by one heavy cloud, that obliterated entirely and forever the sight of that sun which had so long warmed her heart with its genial rays. As we have already said, Komel lacked not for tenderness of feeling. Her heart was gentle and susceptible; but dashing now the tears from her eyes, she assumed a forced calmness, and strove to reason with herself as she said, quietly, "We shall meet again in heaven!" Humming some wild air of her native land, the slave then tried to lose herself in some trifling occupation, that she might partially forget her sorrows.

Her flowers were not forgotten, nor her pet pigeons unattended. She wandered amid the fragrant divisions of the harem, and threw herself down by its bubbling jets and fountains as she had done before, but not thoughtlessly. The spirit of Aphiz seemed to her to be ever by her side, and she would talk to him as though he was actually present, in soft and tender whispers, and sing the songs of their native valley with low and witching cadence; and thus she was partially happy, for the soul is where it loves, rather than where it lives. From childhood she had been taught to believe the Swedenborgian doctrine, of the presence of the spirits of those who have gone before us to the better land; and she deemed, as we have said, that Aphiz Adegah was ever by her side, listening to her, and sympathizing with all she did and said.

It is a happy faith, that the disembodied spirits of those whom we have loved and respected here are still, though invisible, watching over us with tender solicitude. Such a realization must be chastening in its influence, for who would do an unworthy deed, believing his every act visible to those eyes that he had delighted to please on earth? And yet, could we but realize it, there is always one eye, the Infinite and Supreme One, ever upon us, and should we not be equally sensitive in our doings beneath his ever present being?

It was the character of Komel's belief as to the spirits of the departed, that rendered her so calm and resigned, though the Sultan, in his blindness, attributed it to the forgetfulness engendered by time, and smiled to himself to think how quickly the fickle girl had forgotten one whose ardent devotion to her cost him his life. "She scarcely deserved this fidelity on his part," said the monarch, with a dark frown, as the memory of the gallant service the young Circassian had done him when he was beset by the Bedouins, flashed across his mind, rendering even his hardened spirit, for a moment, uneasy. "The difficulty, after all," he said to him himself, "is not so much to die for one we love, as to find one worthy of dying for." Shaking an extra dose of the powdered drug into the bowl of his pipe, the blue smoke curled away in tiny clouds above his head, while its narcotic effect soon lulled both mental and physical faculties into a state of dreamy insensibility.

What ardent spirits are to our countrymen, opium is in the East, except, perhaps that the powerful drug is more exalting in its stimulating influences, and less vile in its immediate effects; but no less severe is it to hurry those who indulge in such dissipation, with a broken constitution and ruined mental faculties to the grave.

Komel seemed gradually to settle down to a quiet and even half satisfied consciousness of her situation. True, she could not but often sigh for her home and parents, but with her more settled condition fresh spirits had come to her features, and renewed energies were depicted in every movement of her graceful and lovely form. Though constantly surrounded by a troop of slaves, chosen solely for their personal beauty and the charms that made them excel their sex generally, still she outshone them all, and that, too, without the simplest effort to do so; and yet for all this, so sweet was her native disposition, and so winning and gentle her spirit at all times, that they loved her still as at first, without one thought of envy or jealousy.

So far as her companions were concerned, therefore, she could hardly have been more happily situated than she was, and for their kindness she strove to manifest the kind, affectionate promptings that actuated her heart. She even joined them in many of their games and sports, though most of her time was passed alone, save that the idiot boy almost ever sought her out, and came and slept at her side, or seemed to do so, only too much delighted when she showed him any little, careful attention, and watching her when she did not observe him, with an intensity that seemed strange in one who was not supposed to be possessed of any actual reasoning powers, or indeed of much brains at all.

Having no mental occupation, the poor boy. who was, as far as his physical developments went, a specimen of rare youthful beauty and grace of form, employed a large portion of his time in such exercises and feats of agility as a sort of animal instinct might lead him to attempt, and thus Komel was often startled by suddenly beholding him dangling by his feet from some lofty cypress, swinging to and fro like a monkey; or to observe him turning a series of summersets, in a broad circle, with such incredible swiftness as to cause all distinctness of his form to be lost, producing a most singular and magical appearance. Then, perhaps, after forming a circle thus on the green sod he would suddenly plunge into its midst, coil himself up like a snail, or put his head between his feet, and thus go to sleep, or lie there as still as though he had been a stone, for hours at a time.

Thus, days and weeks passed on in the same routine of fairy-like scenes, and the Sultan's slaves counted not the time that brought to them but a never varying dull monotony of indolent luxuriance. They had no intellectual pursuits or tastes, and therefore were but sorry companions for one whose native intelligence was so prominent a trait in her character. Thus it was, therefore, having no one with whom she could truly and honestly sympathize, that Komel preferred to whisper her thoughts to the birds and flowers, and to fancy that Aphiz's spirit was near by, smiling upon her the while. What a strange and dreamy life the Circassian was passing in the Sultan's harem!

Komel, it is true, mourned for her liberty, and what caged bird is there that does not!

CHAPTER IX.

THE LOVER'S STRATAGEM.

It was morning in the East, and all things partook of the dewy freshness of early days.—The busy din of the city was momentarily increasing, and as the hours advanced, the broad sunlight gilded all things far and near. It was at this bright and exhilarating hour that two persons sat together on the silky grass that caps the summit of Bulgarlu. They had wandered hither, seemingly, to view the splendid scenery together, and were regarding it with earnest eyes.

How beautiful looked the Turkish capital below them! From Seraglio Point, seven miles down the coast of Roumelia, the eye followed a continued wall, and from the same point twenty miles up the Bosphorus on either shore, stretched one crowded and unbroken city, with its star-shaped bay in the midst, floating a thousand maritime crafts, prominent among which were the Turkish men-of-war flaunting their blood-red flags in the breeze. Far away over the Sea of Mannora their eyes rested on a snow-white cloud at the edge of the horizon. It was Mount Olympus, the fabulous residence of the gods. In this far-off scene, too, lay Bithynia, Cappadocia, Paphlagonia, and the entire scene of the apostle Paul's travels in Asia Minor. Then their eyes wandered back once more and rested now on the old Fortress of the Seven Towers, where fell the emperor Constantine, and where Othman the second was strangled.

Between the Seven Towers and the Golden Horn, were the seven hills of ancient Stamboul, the towering arches of the aqueduct of Valens crossing from one to another, and the swelling domes and gold-tipped minarets of a hundred imperial mosques crowning their summits. And there too was Seraglio Point, a spot of enchanting loveliness, forming a tiny cape as it projects towards the opposite continent and separates the bay from the Sea of Marmora; its palaces buried in soft foliage, out of which gleam gilded cupolas and gay balconies and a myriad of brilliant and glittering domes. And then their eyes ran down the silvery link between the two seas, where lay fifty valleys and thirty rivers, while an imperial palace rests on each of the loveliest spots, the entire length, from the Black Sea to Marmora.

Such was the beautiful and classic scenery that lay outspread before the two young persons who had seated themselves on the summit of Bulgarlu, and if its charms had power over the casual observer, how much more beautiful did it appear to these two who saw it through each other's eyes. A closer observation would have shown that one of the couple was a female, for some purpose seeking to disguise her sex; he by her side was evidently her lover, to meet whom, she had hazarded this exposure beyond the city walls at so early an hour.

"Ah, dearest Zillah'," said he who sat by the maiden's side, "I would that we lived beyond the sea from whence, come those ships that bear the stars and stripes, for I am told that in America, religious belief is no bar to the union of heart, as it is in the Sultan's domains."

"Nor should it be so here, Capt. Selim," she answered, "did our noble Sultan understand the best good of his people. May the Prophet open his eyes."

"Though I love thee far better than all else on the earth, Zillah, still I cannot abjure my Christian faith, and, like a hypocrite, pretend to be a true follower of Mahomet. At best, we can be but a short time here on earth, and if I was unfaithful in my holy creed, how could I hope at last to meet thee, dearest, in paradise?"

"I do love thee but the more dearly," she replied, "for thy constancy to the Christian faith, and though my father has reared me in the Mussulman belief, still I am no bigot, as thou knowest."

Zillah was a child in years—scarcely sixteen summers had developed their power in her slight but beautiful form, and yet it was rounded so nearly to perfection, so slightly and gracefully full, as to captivate the most fastidious eye. Like every child of these Turkish harems, she was beautiful, with feature of faultless regularity, and eyes that were almost too large and brilliant.

He who was her companion, and whom she had called Capt. Selim, was the same young officer whom the reader met in an early chapter at the slave bazaar, and who bid to the extent of his means for Komel, who was at last borne away by the Sultan's agent. He was well formed and handsome, his undress uniform showing him to be attached to the naval service of the Sultan. He might be four or five years her senior, but though he appeared thus young, he seemed to have many years of experience, with an unflinching steadiness of purpose denoted in his countenance, showing him fitted for stern emergencies calling for promptness and daring in the hour of danger. The story of their love was easily told. While young Selim was yet a lieutenant in the Sultan's navy, a caique containing Zillah and the rich of Bey, her father, had met with an accident in the Bosphorus while close by a boat which he commanded, and by which accident Zillah was thrown into the water, and but for the officer's prompt delivery would doubtless have been drowned. But with a stout purpose, and being a daring swimmer, he bore her safely to the shore.

With the suddenness of oriental passion they loved at once, but their after intercourse was necessarily kept a secret, since they knew full well that the Bey would at once punish them both if he should discover them, for how could a Musselman tolerate a Christian, and to this sect the young officer was known to belong. They had met often thus, and by the ingenious device adopted in Zillah's dress had avoided detection. But these stolen meetings, so sweet, were fearfully dangerous to the young officer, the punishment of his offence, if discovered, being death.

Finally, on one of these stolen excursions, Zillah was detained so long as to cause notice and surprise in the harem, and when she returned she was reprimanded by the Bey, who gave orders, that for the future she should not be permitted to leave the garden walks of the palace, and the poor girl pined like a caged wild bird. The latticed balcony of Zillah's apartment, like many of the Turkish houses, overhung the Bosphorus, so that a boat might lie beneath it within a distance to afford easy means of communication, and thus Selim still was able at times, though with the utmost caution, to hold converse with her he loved so well.

But Zillah's susceptible and gentle disposition could not sustain her present treatment. She loved the young officer so earnestly and truly that it was misery to be deprived of his society as was now the case, for even their partial intercourse had been suspended since the Bey had discovered his daughter talking to some one, and he had forbidden her to ever enter the apartment again that overhung the water.

Thus confined and crossed in her feelings, Zillah grew sick, and paler and paler each day, until the old Bey, now thoroughly aroused, was extremely anxious lest she should be taken to the Prophet's house. The best sages and doctors to be found were summoned, and constantly attended the drooping flower, but alas! to no effect. Their art was not cunning enough to discover the true cause of her malady, and they could only shake their heads, and strike their beards ominously to the inquiries of the anxious old Bey, her father.

The cold-hearted Bey never dreamed of the real cause of her illness. True, he had suspected her of being too unguarded in her habits, and had laid restrictions upon her liberty, but as to disappointment in love being the cause of her malady, indeed it did not seem to his heartless disposition that love could produce such a result. She was perhaps the only being in the world who had ever caused him to realize that he had a heart. After thinking long and much upon the illness of his child, he resolved to seek her confidence, and turning his steps toward the harem, he found his drooping and fading flower reclining upon a velvet couch. Seating himself by her side, he parted the hair from her fair, young brow, and told his child how dearly he loved her, and if aught weighed upon her mind he besought her to open her lips and speak to him. Zillah loved her father, though she was not blind to his many faults.

"Dear father, what shall I say to thee?"

"Speak thy whole heart, my child."

"Nay, but it would only displease thee, my father, for me to do so."

"Tell me, Zillah, if thou knowest what it is that sickens thee, and robs thy cheek of its bloom?"

"Father," she answered, with a sigh, "my heart is breaking with unhappy love."

"Love!"

"Ay, I love Selim, he who saved me from drowning in the Bosphorus."

"The Sultan's officer?"

"Yes, father, Capt. Selim."

"Why, child, that young rascal is a notorious dog of a Christian. Do you know it?"

"I know he believes not in the faith of our fathers," she answered, modestly.

The old Turk bit his lips with vexation, but dared not vent the passion he felt in the delicate ear of his sick child. Indeed he had only to look into her pale face to turn the whole current of his anger into pity at the danger he read there.

The old Bey knew the spirit that Zillah had inherited both from himself and from her mother, and that she was fixed in her purpose. She frankly told him that she could never be happy unless Selim was her husband. The father was most sadly annoyed. He referred to the best physicians in the city to know if a malady such as his daughter suffered under, could prove fatal, and they assured him that this had frequently been the case. One, however, to whom he applied, informed the Bey that he knew of a Jewish leech who was famed for curing all maladies arising from depression, physical or mental, and if he desired it, he would send the Jew to his house on the subsequent day, when he would say if he could do her any good as it regarded her illness.

Much as the Mussulman despised the race, still, in the hope of benefiting his child by the man's medical skill, he desired the Armenian physician to send the Jew, as he proposed, on the following day, and paying the heavy fee that these leeches know so well how to charge the rich old Turks, the Bey departed once more to his palace.

At the hour appointed, the Armenian physician despatched the Jewish doctor to the Bey's gates, where he was admitted, and received with as much respect as the Turk could bring his mind to show towards unbelievers, and the business being properly premised, the father told the Jew how his daughter was affected, and asked if he might hope for her recovery.

"With great care and cunning skill, perhaps so," said the Jew, from out his overgrown beard.

"If this can be accomplished through thy means, I make thee rich for life," said the Bey.

"We can but try," said the Jew, "and hope for the best. Lead me to thy daughter."

The Bey conducted the leech to his daughter's apartment, and bidding her tell freely all her pains and ills, left the Jew to study her case, while he retired once more to silent converse with himself.

"You are ill," said the Jew, addressing Zillah, while he seated himself and rested his head upon his staff.

"Yes, I am indeed."

"And yet methinks no physical harm is visible in thy person. The pain is in the heart?"

"You speak truly," said Zillah, with a sigh—"I am very unhappy."

"You love?"

"I do."

"And art loved again?"

"Truly, I believe so."

"Then, whencefore art thou unhappy; reciprocal love begets not unhappiness?"

"True, good leech; but he whom I love so well is a Christian, and I can hold no communication with him, much less even hope to be his wife."

"Do you love him so well that you would leave home, father, everything, for him?" asked the Jew.

"Alas! it would be hard to leave my father but still am I so wholly his, I would do even so."

"Then may you be happy yet," said he, who spoke to her, as he tossed back the hood of his gaberdine, and removed the false hair that he wore, presenting the features of young Selim, whom she loved!

"How is this possible?" she said, between her sobs and smiles of joy; "my father told me that the Armenian recommended you for your skill in the healing art."

"He is my friend, the man who taught me my religion, my everything, and the only confidant I have in all Constantinople. To him I told the grief of my heart at our separation; by chance your father called on him for counsel; he knew the Bey, and his mind suggested that I was the true physician whom you needed, and fabricating the story of my profession, he sent me hither."

The fair young girl gazed at him she loved, and wept with joy, and with her hands held tremblingly in his own, Selim told her of a plan he had formed for their escape from the city to some distant land where they might live together unmolested and happy in each other's society. He explained to her that he should tell her father that it was necessary for him to administer certain medicines to her beneath the rays of the moon, and that while she was strolling with him thus the water's edge, he would have a boat ready and at a favorable moment jumping into this, they would speed away.

The moments flew with fearful speed, and pressing her tenderly to his heart, the pretended Jew had only time to resume his disguise when the Bey entered. He saw in the face of his child a color and spirit that had not been there for months before, and delighted, he turned to the Jew to know if he had administered any of his cunning medicines, and being told that a small portion of the necessary article had been given, was overjoyed at the effect.

Being of a naturally superstitious race, the Turk heard the Jew's proposition as it regarded the administering of his next dose of medicine beneath the calm rays of the moon in the open air, with satisfaction; for had he not already worked a miracle upon his child? He was told that by administering the medicine once or twice at the proper moment beneath the midnight rays of the moon, he should doubtless be able to effect a perfect cure.

Satisfied fully of what he had seen and heard, he dismissed the pretended Jew with a heavy purse of gold, and bade him choose his own time, telling him also that his palace gates should ever be open to him.

CHAPTER X.

THE SERENADE.

Beautiful as a poet's fancy can picture, is the seraglio, a fitting home for the proud Turkish monarch, gemmed with gardens, fantastic palaces, and every variety of building and tree on its gentle slope, descending so gracefully towards the sea, spreading before the eye its towers, domes, and dark spots of cypresses like a sacred division of the city of Constantinople, as indeed it is to the eye of the true believer.

The Sultan's household were removed at his will from the Valley of Sweet Waters hither and back again, as fancy might dictate. Thus Komel had met her lover Aphiz Adegah here before his sentence; and here she was now, still queen of its royal master's heart, still the fairest creature that shone in the Sultan's harem. Every luxury and beauty that ingenuity could devise or wealthy purchase, surrounded her with oriental profusion. Still left entirely to herself, the same occupation employed her time, of tending flowers and toying with beautiful birds. Sometimes the Sultan would come and sit by her side, but he found that the wound he had given was not one to heal so quickly as he had supposed, and that the Circassian cherished the memory of Aphiz as tenderly as ever.

The idiot boy, almost the only person in whom she seemed to take any real interest, still followed her footsteps hither and thither, now toying with some pet of the gardens, a parrot or a dog, now performing most incredible feats of legerdemain, running off upon his hands, with his feet in a perpendicular position, to a distance, and coming back again by a series of summersets, until suddenly gathering his limbs and body together like a ball, he went off rolling like a helpless mass down some gentle slope, and having reached the bottom, would lie there as if all life were gone, for the hour together, yet always so managing as to keep one eye upon Komel nearly all the while.

The Circassian loved the poor half-witted boy, for love begets love, and the lad had seemed to love her from the first moment they had met in the Sultan's halls, since when they had been almost inseparable.

It was on a fair summer's afternoon, that the Sultan, strolling in the flower gardens of the palace, either by design or accident, came upon a spot where Komel was half reclining upon one of the soft lounges that were strewn here and there under tiny latticed pagodas, to shelter the occupant from the sun. While yet a considerable way off, the Turk paused to admire his slave as she reclined there in easy and unaffected gracefulness, apparently lost in a day dream. She was very beautiful there all by herself, save the half-witted boy, who seemed to be asleep now, away out on the projecting limb of a cypress tree that nearly overhung the spot, and where he had coiled himself up, and managed to sustain his position upon the limb by some unaccountable means of his own.

The Sultan drew quietly nearer until he was close by her side before she discovered him, when starting from the reverie that had bound her so long, she half rose out of respect for the monarch's presence, but no smile clothed her features; she welcomed him not by greeting of any kind.

"What dreams my pretty favorite about, with her eyes open all the while?" asked the Sultan.

"How knew you that I dreamed?"

"I read it in your face. It needs no conjuror to define that, Komel."

"Would you know of what I was thinking?"

"It was my question, pretty one."

"Of home—of my poor parents, and of my lost Aphiz," she answered, bitterly.

"I have told thee to forget those matters, and content thyself here as mistress of my harem."

"That can never be; my heart to-day is as much as ever among my native hills."

"Well, Komel, time must and will change you, at last. We are not impatient."

The Circassian Slave

Had the monarch rightly interpreted the expression of her face at this moment, he would have understood how deeply rooted was her resolve, at least, so far as he was concerned, and that she bitterly despised the murderer of Aphiz, and in this spirit only could she look upon the proud master of the Turkish nation. He mistook Komel's disposition and nature, in supposing that she would ever forgive or tolerate him. He did not remember how unlike her people she had already proved herself. He did not realize that his high station, his wealth, the pomp and elegance that surrounded his slave, were looked upon by her only as the flowers that adorn the victim of a sacrifice. Having never been thwarted in his will and purpose, he had yet to learn that such a thing could be accomplished by a simple girl.

As the Sultan turned an angle in the path that led towards the palace, he was met by one of the eunuch guards, who saluted him after the military style with his carbine, and marched steadily on in pursuance of his duty. The monarch did not even lift his eyes at the guard's salute—his thoughts were uneasy, and his brow dark with disappointment.

It was but a few hours subsequent to the scene which we have just described, that Komel was again seated in the seraglio gardens on the gentle slope where it curves towards the sea. She had wandered beneath the bright stars and silvery moon as far as it was prudent for her to do, and cleft only the narrow path trod by the silent guard between her and the wall of the seraglio. The hour was so late that stillness reigned over the moon-lit capital, and the place was as silent as the deep shadows of night. The half-witted boy had followed her steps by swinging himself from tree to tree, until now he was close by the spot where she sat, though lost to sight among the thick foliage of the funereal cypress.

Komel was thinking of the strange vicissitudes of her life, of her lost lover, of the dear cottage where she was born, and the happy home from which she had been so ruthlessly torn by violent hands. It was an hour for quiet thoughtfulness, and her innocent bosom heaved with almost audible motion as it realized the scene and her own memories. She sat and looked up at those bright lamps hung in the blue vault above her, until her eyes ached with the effort, and now the train of thoughts in which she had indulged, at last started the pearly drops upon her check, and dimmed her eyes. It was not often that she gave way to tears, but her thoughts, the scene about her, and everything, seemed to have combined to touch her tenderest sensibilities.

In this mood, breathing the soft and gentle night breeze, she gradually lost her consciousness, and fell asleep as quietly as a babe might have done in its cradle, and presented a picture as pure and innocent.

She dreamed, too, of home and all its happy associations. Once more, in fancy, she was by her own cottage door; once more she breathed her native mountain air, once more sat by the side of Aphiz, her loved, dearly loved companion. Ah! how her dimpled cheeks were wreathed in smiles while she slept; how happy and unconscious was the beautiful slave. And now she seems to hear the song of her native valley falling upon her ear as Aphiz used to sing it. Hark! is that delusion, or do those sounds actually fall upon her waking ear? Now she rouses, and like a startled fawn listens to hear from whence come those magic notes, and by whom could they be uttered. She stood electrified with amazement.

And still there fell upon her ear the song of her native hills, breathed in a soft, low chant, to the accompaniment of a guitar, and in notes that seemed to thrill her very soul while she listened.

They came evidently from beyond the seraglio wall, and from some boatman on the river. Then a sort of superstitious awe crept over the slave as she remembered that it was in these very waters that Aphiz had been drowned. Had his spirit come back to sing to her the song they had so often sung together? Thus she thought while she listened, and still the same sweet familiar notes came daintily over the night air to her ears. The only spot that commanded a view beyond the wall was occupied by the sentinel, and Komel could not gratify the almost irresistible desire to satisfy herself with her own eyes from whence these well remembered notes came. It was either Aphiz's spirit, or the voice of one born and bred among her native hills—of this she felt assured.

So marked was her excitement, and so peculiar her behaviour, that the guard seemed at last aroused to take notice of the affair, and in his ignorance of the circumstances, presumed that the serenader, who could be seen in a small boat on the river from the spot where he stood, was attempting some intrigue with the Sultan's people, and knowing well the object of his being placed there was to prevent such things, he took particular note of both the slave and the serenader for many minutes, until at last, satisfied of the correctness of his surmise, he resolved to gain for himself some credit with his officer, by making an example of the venturesome boatman, whoever he might be.

Where the sentinel stood, as we have said, he could command a perfect view of the spot from whence the song came, and also discern the serenader himself. He saw him, too, pull the little egg-shell caique in which he sat still nearer the wall of the seraglio. Komel, too, had observed the guard, and now perceived that it was evident by his actions that he saw some tangible form from whence came that dear song; and as she saw him deliberately raise and aim his carbine towards that direction, she could not suppress an involuntary scream as she beheld the Turkish guard preparing to shoot probably some native of her own dear valley.

There had been another though silent observer of this scene, and as he heard the cry from Komel's lips, he dropped himself from the tree under which the sentry stood, right upon his shoulders, bearing him to the ground, while the contents of the carbine were cast into the air harmlessly. The half-witted boy had destroyed the aim, and the alarm given by the report of his carbine enabled the boatman, whoever he was, to make good his escape at once. The enraged guard turned to vent his anger upon the cause of his failure to kill the boatman, but when he beheld the half-witted being gazing up at the stars as unconcernedly as though nothing had happened, he remembered that the person of the boy was sacred.

With a suppressed oath the guard resumed his weapon, and paced along the path that formed his post.

As soon as the excitement attendant upon the scene we have related had subsided, Komel once more turned in wonder to recall those sweet notes, so endeared to her by a thousand associations, and to wonder from whom and whence they came. Was it possible that some dear friend from home had discovered her prison, her gilded cage, and that those notes were intended for her ear, or had the singer, by some miraculous chance, come hither and uttered those notes thoughtlessly? Thus conjecturing and surmising, Komel scarcely closed her eyes all night, and when she did so, it was to live over in her dreams the scenes we have referred to, and to seem to hear once more those thrilling and tender notes of her far off home.

Then she seemed once more to behold the Turk taking his deadly aim, and the idiot boy dropping from the tree to frustrate his murderous intention, and throwing the guard by his weight to the ground; and then the imaginary report of the carbine would again arouse her, to fall asleep and dream once more.

During the whole of the day that followed she could think of nothing but that strange serenade; she even thought of the possibility of her father having traced her hither, and sung that song to ascertain if she were there, and then she wondered that she had not thought on time instant to reply to it, and resolved on the subsequent evening to watch if the song should be repeated, resolving that if this was the case, to respond to its notes come from whom they might. And with this purpose, a little before the same hour, she repaired thither with her light guitar hung by a silken cord by her neck.

But in vain did she listen and watch for the song to be repeated. All was still on those beautiful waters, and no sound came upon the ear save the distant burst of delirious mirth from some opium shop where the frequenters had reached a state of wild and noisy hilarity, under the influence of the intoxicating drug. The half-witted boy seemed to comprehend her wishes, and already with a leap that would have done credit to a greyhound, had thrown himself on the top of the seraglio wall on the sea side, and sat there, watching first Komel, and then the water beneath the point.

Despairing at last of again hearing the song, she lightly struck the strings of her guitar, and thus accompanied, sung the song that she had heard the previous night. The boy recognized the first note of the air, and springing to his feet, peered off into the shadows upon the water, supposing they came from thence; but seeing by a glance that it was the slave who sung, he dropped from the wall and crept quietly to her side. Before the song was ended he lay down at her feet in a state apparently of dormancy, though his eyes, peering from beneath one of his arms, were fixed upon a cluster of stars that shone the heavens above him.

The bell from an English man-of-war that lay but an arrow's shot off, had sounded the middle watch before Komel left the spot where she had hoped once more to hear those to her enchanting sounds. She arose and walked away with reluctant steps from the place towards the palace, leaving the idiot boy by himself. But scarcely had she gone from sight, before he jumped to his feet, leaped once more to the top of the wall, looked off with apparent earnestness among the shipping and along the shore of the sparkling waters, where the moon lay in long rays of silver light upon it, and then dropping once more to the ground, came to the spot where Komel had sat, and lying down there, slept, or seemed to do so.

Here Komel came night after night, but the song was no more repeated. Either the sentry's shot had effectually frightened away the serenader, or else he had not come hither with any fixed object connected with his song. In either case the poor girl felt unhappy and disappointed in the matter, and her companions saw a cloud of care upon her fair face. The Sultan, too, marked this, and seemed to wonder that time did not heal the wounded spirit of his slave. His kindly endeavors to please and render her content bore no fruit of success. She avoided him now; the feeling of gratitude that she had at first entertained towards him, had given way to one of deep but silent hatred.

The monarch could read as much in her face whenever they chanced to meet, and the feelings of tenderness which he had entertained for her were also changing, and he felt that he should soon exercise the right of a master if he could make no impression upon the beautiful Circassian as a lover.

"You treat me with coldness, Komel," he said to her, reproachfully.

"Our actions are only truthful when they speak the language of the heart," replied she.

"You forget my forbearance."

"I forget nothing, but remember constantly too much," she replied.

"It may be, Komel, that you do not remember on thing, which it is necessary to recall to you mind. You are my slave!"

Leaving the Sultan and his household, we will turn once more to Capt. Selim, and see with what success he treated his fair patient, the old Bey's daughter, in his assumed character of a Jewish leech.

CHAPTER XI.

THE ELOPEMENT.

The palace of the old Bey, Zillah's father, was one of those gilded, pagoda-like buildings, which, in any other climate or any other spot in the wide world, would have looked foolish, from its profusion of latticed external ornaments, and the filagree work that covered every angle and point, more after the fashion of a child's toy than the work most appropriate for a dwelling house. But here, on the banks of the Bosphorus, in sight of Constantinople, and within the dominion of that oriental people, it was appropriate in every belonging, and seemed just what a Turkish palace should be.

The building extended so over the water that its owner could drop at once into his caique and be pulled to almost any part of the city, and, like all the people who live along the river's banks, he was much on its surface. Coiled away, a la Turk, with his pipe well supplied, a pull either to the Black Sea, or that of Marmora, with a dozen stout oarsmen, was a delightful way of passing an afternoon, returning as the twilight hour settled over the scene.

It was perhaps a week subsequent to the time when Selim and Zillah met at the Bey's house, availing himself of the liberty so fully extended by her father, Selim, in his disguise as a Jew, again appeared at the palace gate, where he was received with a request and consideration that showed to him he was expected, and at his request he was conducted to the Bey's presence, and by him, again to the apartment where his daughter was reposing.—The pretended Jew followed his guide with the most profound sobriety, handling sundry vials and jars he had brought with him, and upon which the Bey looked with not a little interest and respect, as he strove to decipher the cabalistic lines on each.

"Have you found any improvement in the malady that affects your child?" asked the Jew, pouring a part of the contents of one vial into another, and holding it up against the light, exhibiting a phosphorescent action in the vial.

"By the beard of the prophet, yes; a marked and potent change has your wonderful medicines produced. But what use do you make of that strange compound that looks like liquid fire?"

"'Tis a strange compound," answered the other, seeming to regard the mixture with profound interest; "very strange. Perhaps you would hardly believe it, but the contents of that vial cast into the Bosphorus, would kill every fish below your latticed windows to the Dardanelles."

"Allah Akbar!" exclaimed the credulous Turk, holding up both hands. "And this medicine, so powerful, do you intend for one so delicate as she?" he asked, pointing to Zillah, who was reclining upon a pile of cushions.

"I do; but with that judicious, care that forms the art of our profession. So peculiar is the means that I shall operate with to-night, that should it harm her, it would equally affect me. But I have studied her case well, and you will find when yonder fair moon now rising from behind the hills of Scutari shall sink again to rest, your daughter will be well."

"Then will I stop and watch the wonderful operation of thy drugs."

"Nay, they must be applied in the open air and beneath the moon's rays, with none to observe, save the stars."

"Then may the Prophet protect you. I will leave my child in your care. Shall I do this, Zillah?"

"Father, yes, with thy blessing first," said the fair girl; for well she knew, that the medicine which was to cure her, would carry her away from his side and her childhood home, perhaps forever.

The Bey pressed his lips to her forehead, and with a curious glance at the strange jars and vials, which the pretended Jew had displayed, he turned away and left them together.

"Ah, dearest Zillah," said Selim, as soon as he found himself alone with her he loved, "all is prepared as I promised thee, and at midnight we will leave this palace forever."

"Alas! dear Selim, my heart is ever with thee, but it is very sad to turn away from these scenes among which I have grown up from infancy; but full well I know I can never be thine otherwise."

"In time your father will be reconciled to us both, Zillah, and then we may return again," said the disguised lover, striving to re-assure the gentle girl, whose heart almost failed her.

"But what a fearful risk you incur even now," she said; "your disguise once discovered, Selim, and to-morrow's sun would never shine upon you; your life would be forfeited."

"Fear not for me, dearest. I am well versed in the part I am to play. But come, it is already time for us to walk forth in the moonlight. Clothe thyself thoughtfully, Zillah, for your dress must be such as will suffice you for many days, since we must fly far away over the sea, beyond the reach of pursuit."

"I will be thoughtful," answered the gentle girl, retiring a few moments from his side.

They wandered on among the fairy-like scenes of the garden, where the trees overhung the Bosphorus, repeating once more the story of their love, and renewing those oft-repeated promises of eternal fidelity, until nearly midnight, when Selim suddenly started as he heard the low, muffled sound of oars. He paused but for a moment, then hastily seizing upon Zillah's arm, he urged her to follow him quickly to the water's edge. Throwing a heavy, long military cloak about her, he completely screened her from all eyes, and placing her in the stern of the boat that came for him, with a wave of the hand he bade his men give way, while he steered the caique towards a craft that lay up the river towards the city, and soon disappeared among the forest of masts and shipping that lay at anchor off Seraglio Point.

They had made good their escape at least for the present, and were safe on board the ship commanded by Captain Selim. The very boldness of his scheme would prevent him from being discovered, and neither feared that the ship of the Sultan would be searched at any event, to find the lost daughter of the old Bey.

On the subsequent day the old Bey summoned his royal master to assist him to find his child. The Armenian doctor, who recommended the pretended Jew, was called upon to explain matters, but, to the astonishment of the Turk, he denied in toto any knowledge of what he referred to, declared before the Sultan that he had neither offered to send any one to the Bey's house, nor had he done so, nor did he know a single Jewish leech in the capital.

Confounded at such a flat contradiction, and having not the least evidence to rebut it, the Turk was obliged to withdraw from the royal presence discomfited, while the Armenian doctor retired to his own dwelling, comforting himself, in the first place, if he had uttered a falsehood it was in a good cause; and next, that he held it no crime to deceive or to cheat an infidel, and ever one knows how little love exists between the Turks and Armenians, at Constantinople.

The truth was that the Armenian had long known Selim, had taught him his religion, and, had instructed him much at various times in such matters as it behooved him to know, and which had placed him at an early age far above many others in the service, who had all sorts of favoritism to advance their interests. He knew of Selim's love for the old Bey's daughter, and when chance led the father to consult him about his child, the idea of sending Selim to his house, as he succeeded in doing, flashed across his mind, and he proposed it to the father, as we have seen.

Selim's Armenian friend repaired on board his vessel as soon as he was released from the presence of the Sultan, upon the inquiry to which we have alluded. It would have gone hard with him had it not been that his skill in his profession had long since recommended him to the Sultan, in whose household he frequently appeared. Selim greeted him kindly, and told him he was indebted to him for his future happiness in life.

"We have been so successful in this plan," said the Armenian, "that I have half a mind to try one of a similar, but far bolder character, if you will assist me."

"With all my heart. What is it you propose?" asked Captain Selim.

"In my visits to the Sultan's harem, I have more than once been brought—"

"Is the attempt to be made upon the Sultan's harem?" interrupted Selim.

"Be patient and hear my story."

"I will, but this must be a bold business."

"I say, in my visits to the Sultan's household, I have often been brought in contact with one whom I know to be very unhappy, and who is detained there against her will. She is queen, I think, not only of the harem, but also of its master's heart, her beauty and bearing being of surpassing loveliness. Her history, too, as far as I can learn, is one of romantic interest, and she pines to return to her home in Circassia, from whence she was violently torn. At first when she came here, I was called upon to treat her case, for she had lately recovered from some severe sickness, and I then saw how tenderly the Sultan regarded her. Well, at that time she was both deaf and dumb, but—"

"Hold! do you say she was deaf and dumb?" asked Selim, as if he recalled some memory of the past.

"I did."

"Strange," mused the officer; "it must be the slave that I bid for in the market."

And so indeed it was the same beautiful being who had so earnestly attracted him, as the reader will remember, when the Sultan's agent, Mustapha, overbid him in the bazaar.

"You know her then?" asked the Armenian.

"I think so; but go on."

"Well, I am satisfied that she pines to be released, and from hearing her story, and tending her in a short illness, I have become deeply interested in her. You know, Selim, that I hate the Turks in my heart, and if I can by any means rob the Sultan of this girl, and restore her to her home, I would risk much to do so."

"The very idea looks to me like an impossibility," answered the young officer.

"Nothing is impossible where will and energy combine."

"What is your plan?"

"You have resolved to fly from here, you tell me at least, by to-morrow night."

"Yes. I have purchased that skimmer of the waters, the Petrel, and I shall sail at that time with Zillah, for the Russian coast, or Trebizond on the south of the Black Sea."

"Very good; now why not take this gentle slave of the Sultan's along with you?"

"But how to get possession of her? that's the question," answered Selim.

"You know I have free access to the palace, and could easily inform her of any plan for her release."

"One half of the trouble is over then at once, if she will second your efforts."

"Well, I will visit the harem this very day. I have good excuse for doing so, and will tell Komel—"

"Komel!" interrupted Selim.

"Yes, that it the slave's name; why, what makes you look so thoughtful?"

"I do not know," said Selim; "the name sounded familiar to me at first, but go on."

"Well, I will tell her what is proposed, and get her advice as to any mode that she may think best to adopt in regard to her escaping."

"But do you think she would prefer to go with me to an uncertain home, to the luxury she enjoys?"

"Of course you will take her to her home on the Circassian coast. That must be the understanding, and I will remunerate you for the extra trouble and expense."

"Never!" said the officer, honestly. "These Turks have paid me well for my services, and I have already a purse heavy with gold, after purchasing the Petrel, and if need be, I can make her pay."

"Have it as you will; it matters not to me, so that she reaches her home, and the Turk is foiled."

"I am a rover myself, and the Circassian coast would suit me quite as well as any other for a season. From whence does she come?"

"Anapa."

"Anapa? that shall be my destination," said Selim, at once.

"Hark! what is that?" asked the physician, turning to the back part of the cabin.

"Nothing, but a young friend of mine; he's asleep, I think."

"Asleep; why he's moving, and must have overheard us, I am sure."

"No fear."

"But what we have said is no more nor less than downright treason."

"That's true."

"And would cost us both our heads if it should be reported."

"He wont report it if he has heard it; he bears the Sultan no good-will, I can assure you, for it is only a day or two since that he was sentenced to death by him for some trivial cause."

"What was it?" asked the Armenian.

"Getting a peep at some of his favorites, I believe, or some such affair."

"Do you remember his name?" asked the Armenian, as the subject of this conversation came out of one of the state-rooms in the cabin, and approached them.

"Yes; he is a Circassian, named Aphiz Adegah!"

CHAPTER XII.

THE STRUGGLE FOR LIFE.

Though to the Armenian physician the fact of Aphiz's being there was nothing remarkable, to the reader we must explain how such a circumstance could be possible after the scenes we have described; for it will be remembered that we left him at the moment he was sunk in the Bosphorus and left by the officers of the Sultan to drown.

The fact was that the Circassian's sentence was more than usually peremptory and sudden, and he was taken at once from the place of confinement and borne away in the boat without his person being searched, or indeed any of the usual precautions in such cases being adopted to prevent accident or the escape of the prisoner. Aphiz submitted without resistance to be placed in the sack, preparatory to being cast into the sea, nor was he ignorant of the fate that was intended to be inflicted upon him, but some confident hope, nevertheless, seemed to support him at the time.

The officers of the prison, not a little surprised at his quiet acquiescence to all their purposes, when all was prepared, cast him, as we have already described, into the sea, and quietly pulled away from the spot. But no sooner did Aphiz find himself immersed in the water than he commenced to cut the bag with his dagger, which he had concealed in his bosom, and as he sank deeper and deeper towards the bottom, quickly to release himself from the restraint of the heavy canvas bag and shot that bore him still down, down, to the fearful depth of the river's bed.

Aphiz Adegah was born near the sea-shore, and from childhood had been accustomed to the freest exercise in the water. He was therefore an expert and well-practised swimmer, and after he had freed himself from the sack by the vigorous use of his dagger, he gradually rose again to the surface of the water, but taking good care to start away from the spot where he had been cast into the sea, that he might not be observed by those who had been sent there to execute the sentence of death upon him.

Still starting away and swimming under water, he gradually rose to the surface far from the spot where he had first sunk, but after a breath, still fearing detection, he dove again, and deeper and deeper, sought to follow the current, until he should be beyond the possibility of discovery. What a volume of thoughts passed through his mind in the few seconds while he was descending in that fearful confinement of the sack, and how vigorously he worked with the edge of his dagger to cut an opening for escape, and when he drew that one long inspiration as he rose to the surface and instantly plunged again, what a relief it was to his aching lungs and overtasked powers! But, as we have said, he was a practised swimmer, knew well his powers, and confidently dove again into the depth of the waters.

As he sank deeper and deeper in this second dive, he found himself suddenly losing all power and control over his body, and he felt as though some invisible arm had seized upon him, and he was being borne away he knew not whither. No effort of his was of the least avail, and on, on, he was borne, and round and round he was turned with the velocity of lightning, until he grew dizzy and faint, and the density of the waters, acting upon the drums of his ears, became almost insupportably painful, imparting a sensation as though the head was between two iron plates, and a screw was being turned which compressed it tighter and tighter every moment.

Though he was in this situation not more than one minute, yet it seemed to him to be an hour of torture, so intense was the agony experienced; and yet it was beyond a doubt his salvation in the end, for he had by chance struck one of those violent undertows that prevail in all these fresh water inland seas, which defy all philosophical calculation, and which bore him with the speed of an arrow for two hundred rods far away from the spot where he had a second time sunk below the surface, until, as he once more rose to the surface, he found himself so far away from the boat that he could not possibly be recognized.

Close by him he heard the strokes and saw the oars of a large man-of-war boat passing by the spot where he had risen from his fearful contest with the water. His first impulse was to dive once more, but his efforts with the current he had struck below had seemed to deprive him of the power of all further exertion. The shore was a quarter of a mile distant, and in his exhausted state, he doubted if it was possible for him to reach it. He gave a second look at the boat with longing eyes, his strength was momentarily failing him, he felt that he must either sink or call to those in the boat for assistance, and while he was thus debating in his own mind, he observed the person who had the helm steer the boat towards him, and in a moment after Aphiz was raised in the arms of the sea men and placed in the bottom of the caique.

Scarcely had he been placed in this position when there commenced throughout his whole system such a combination of fearful and harrowing pains that he almost prayed that he might die, and be relieved from them. He had not the power left in his limbs to move one inch, and yet he felt as though he could roll and writhe all over the boat. The fact was that while exertion was necessary to preserve him from drowning, his instinct and mental faculties combined to support him, and enable the sufferer still to make an effort to preserve his life, but now that no exertion on his part could benefit himself, he was thrown back upon a realization of the consequent suffering induced by his exposure.

The quantity of water he had swallowed pained him beyond measure, while the action of the dense water upon his brain, and the combined pains he was enduring, rendered him almost deranged. It is said that drowning is the easiest of deaths, but those who have recovered from a state nearly approaching actual death by submersion in the water, describe the sensations of recovery to consciousness to be beyond description, painful and terrible. Those who have for a moment fainted from some sudden cause have partially realized this misery in the anguish caused for an instant by the first breath that accompanies returning consciousness.

All this proved too much for the young Circassian, and though removed from the immediate cause of danger he fainted with exhaustion. He who commanded the boat was also a young man, and seemed at once to be uncommonly interested in the stranger whom he had rescued from the sea. Neither he nor any of his men suspected how the half drowned man had come there, and adopting such means as his experience suggested, the officer of the boat soon again restored Aphiz to a state of painful consciousness. Realizing the kind efforts that were made for him, the young Circassian smiled through the trembling features of his face in acknowledgement.

Signing to his men to give way with more speed, the officer soon moored along side one of the Sultan's sloops-of-war, and in a few moments after the half drowned man was placed in the best berth the cabin afforded.

As to himself, Aphiz had only sufficient consciousness left to realize that he had been most miraculously save from a watery grave, but a bare thought of the suffering he had just passed through, was almost too much for him. And leaving chance to decide his future fate, he turned painfully in his cot and was soon lost in sleep.

When the young Circassian awoke on the following morning he was once more quite himself, being thoroughly refreshed by the long hours he had slept. He thought over the last few days which had been so eventful to him, and wondered what fate was now in store for him.—Of course the generous conduct of Captain Selim, the Sultan's officer, who had rescued him from drowning, and then hospitably entertained him, was the most spontaneous action of a noble heart towards a fellow-being in distress, but if he should know by what means Aphiz had come in the situation which he had found him, would not his loyalty to the Sultan demand that he should at once render up the escaped prisoner once more to the executioner's hands?

His true policy therefore seemed to be to keep his own secret, and this he resolved to do, but he had reasoned without knowing the character or feelings of him to whom he was so much indebted, as we shall see.

Scarcely had he resolved the matter in his mind, as we have described, when Selim entered the cabin, and perceiving the refreshed and cheerful appearance of Aphiz, addressed him in a congratulatory tone.

"I rejoice to see you so well."

"Thanks to your prompt assistance and hospitality that I am not now at the bottom of the Bosphorus."

"You were pretty close upon drowning, and must have been under water for some time, I should say."

"I had indeed, and was very nearly exhausted," answered Aphiz.

"But how came you in such a pitiable plight, what led you so far from the shore without a boat?"

"I—that is to say—"

"O, I see, some matter that you wish to keep a secret. Very well; far be it from me to ask aught of thee, or urge thee to reveal any matter that might compromise thy feelings."

"Not so," answered Aphiz; "but were I to speak, I might criminate myself."

"O, fear no such matter with me, were you an escaped prisoner from the law, I—"

"What?" asked Aphiz, as he observed the young officer regarding him intently.

"Why, I should not betray you again into the Sultan's power. I have no real sympathy with these Turks, and would much rather serve you, who seem to be a stranger, than them."

"Thanks, a thousand thanks," answered Aphiz, warmly.

"Therefore, confide in me, and if I can serve thee, I will do so at once."

"I will," said Aphiz, who felt that the officer was honest in what he promised.

Then he told him how he had been condemned by the Sultan, for some private enmity, to die, but he carefully observed the utmost secrecy as to what the actual motive of his punishment really was. He told how he had been borne in the execution boat to the usual spot for the execution of the sentence that had been pronounced upon him. How he had been confined in the sack and cast into the sea, describing his first sensations and his struggle with his dagger until he cut himself free from the terrible confinement of his canvas prison. How he had struggled beneath the element, and then of the fearful eddy into which he had been drawn, and finally how at last he rose to the surface near his own boat.

That was all that Captain Selim knew of the matter, and after hearing that Aphiz was a Circassian, he supplied him with an undress uniform to further his disguise, and bade him welcome as his guest. Therefore when the Armenian doctor and Selim found that their conversation had been overheard by Aphiz, they neither feared his betraying him, nor suspected the deep interest that the young Circassian felt in the theme of their remarks.

"You were speaking of a slave of the Sultan's harem, named Komel," he said, approaching them.

"We were; and perhaps have spoken too plainly of a purpose for her release from bondage," said the Armenian.

"Why too freely?"

"Because in a degree we have placed ourselves in your power, having spoken treason."

"I care not whether it be treason or not," replied Aphiz; "it was such as answered to the feelings of my own heart in every word. Betray you! I will die to achieve the object you name."

"This is singular," said Selim, surprised at his earnestness.

"It would not seem so had I dared to tell you my story at first."

"Then you know the girl?" asked the physician and Selim, in a breath.

"Know her? I have been her playmate from childhood. We have loved and cherished each other until our very souls seemed blended into one."

"Then how came she separated from you, and now in the Sultan's harem?" asked the Armenian.

"Ay," continued Selim, "how was it that I saw her offered for sale in the public bazaar?"

"Have patience with me and I will tell you all, of both her history and my own."

Aphiz then related to them the story that is already familiar to the reader, and seeing that those with whom he had to deal were in no way particularly partial to the Sultan, he told word for word the whole truth, even from the hour when he had saved him from the Bedouins, to that when he had been cast into the sea.

All this but the more incited both Selim and the Armenian to strive for Komel's release, and sitting there together, the trio strove how best they could manage the affair. The Armenian's possessing the entree to the palace was a matter of intense importance to the furtherance of the object, and whatever plan should be adopted it was agreed that he should seek the harem and communicate it to Komel, thus obtaining her aid in its execution.

"Doubtless she thinks me dead," said Aphiz; "for the Sultan would take care to tell her that."

"That's true, and so let her think, and we will manage an agreeable surprise for her."

"As you will; but let us to this business this very night," said the impatient Aphiz.

"That we will, and right heartily," said Selim, who hastened to his young wife to tell her that she was to have a dear, beautiful companion in their proposed voyage, and that she would be on board before the morning.

Aphiz was now all impatience. He could scarcely wait for the hours to pass that should bring about the period allotted for the attempt to release her whom he so fondly, and until now so hopelessly, loved. In the meantime the good Armenian physician, with redoubled interest, now that he had learned Aphiz's story, sought the Sultan's harem, where he quietly broached to Komel the plan that had been agreed upon whereby she should be transported once more to her distant home and the scenes of her childhood.

CHAPTER XIII.

THE ESCAPE FROM THE HAREM.

On one of those soft and glorious nights such as occur so often beneath the eastern skies, when there was no moon and yet a blaze of light pouring down from the myriad of bright stars, that one would not have missed the absence of the Queen of Night; the walks of the Sultan's gardens, fragrant with flowers and sweet blossoms, were drinking in of the dewy hour, still and silently, save at the point where we once before introduced the person of Komel. The spot from whence she had listened to that tender and dearly loved song of her native valley, and nearly in the same place she sat now, again evidently listening and expecting the coming of some person or preconcerted signal.

On the extended branch of the nearest cypress hung the half-witted boy by one arm, which he had cast over the limb, and from whence he was now oscillating like a pendulum, his head hanging down upon his breast, and the rest of his limbs as moveless seemingly, as though he had hung there for months. It was one of the queer odd freaks that he was so often performing, for what purpose no one knew, and there he hung still, while the slave listened and cast anxious glances at the stone wall that forms the sea side of the seraglio gardens.

But no sound greeted her ears save the never ceasing babbling of the fountains, and now and then the soft plaintive cry of some night bird that, wakeful while most of the species slept, warbled its notes to the stars. Once she thought she heard the muffled sound of oars, and started to her feet, but the noise soon died away in the distance, and she relapsed again into the same attitude of impatient and anxious anticipation. Out from under the apparently drooping and senseless eyelids of the idiot, a quick thoughtful glance was turned upon her at every motion she made, but she knew it not, nor did she turn towards the boy at all, while he still swung steadily as though he had been bound by cords to the tree.

Once more she started, but it was a false alarm. The notes she had heard were those of an instrument, played by some favorite of the harem, who looked forth upon the night scene, and coupled its

97

charms with the notes of her lute.—But this too soon died away, and again Komel breathed quick and anxiously as she sat there at midnight. The guard on his rounds came past now, and she assumed a quiet and careless air to avoid notice, while a soldier cast a wondering eye at the idiot boy, and then strode on, with the barrel of his carbine resting lazily in the hollow of his arm.

At this moment there swelled forth upon the night air the note of that well remembered song. It was the preconcerted signal, and springing to her feet, Komel stole quickly to that part of the seraglio wall nearest the water. The idiot boy seemed to comprehend the movement instantly, and to recognize the notes that he had heard once before, and which had so affected the beautiful Circassian, nor had she fairly reached the wall before he was close by her side. She paused for a moment to smile kindly upon him and place her hand upon his head, then turned to listen again.

The boy appeared to understand that something extraordinary was going on, and became as nervous as possible. Now he darted off towards the path where the sentinel had disappeared, and now came back with a step as fleet as a deer, and as noiseless as a cat's. But the scene soon changed by the appearance, above the wall, of the head of Captain Selim, who, peering carefully around for a moment, asked in a whispered tone:

"Lady, lady, are you there?"

"I am," replied Komel, cautiously, while the idiot crowded close to her side.

"If I throw over this rope ladder, will you mount now to the top of the wall?"

"Yes, O yes; let me get away from here quickly."

"Step away from the wall then for a moment," said the young officer, and in an instant after a rope ladder made fast on the outer side, was cast over to her.

"Are you ready, lady?"

"Yes."

"Then come quickly; don't pause for a moment in the ascent, lest you be seen."

Komel thinking of nothing but release from her confinement in the Sultan's household, and seeing in perspective her home and parents, for the Armenian had promised that she should be taken thither, sprang lightly up the tiny, but strong ladder of cord, and was soon on the other side, the boy creeping after as she went. But just as she had passed over the top and was descending on the other side, leaving the idiot boy on the top beside of the young officer, who stood so that his neck and head were above the level of the summit of the wall, the sentinel again came down the path in sight of the place and instantly discovered the whole affair, running with all speed to the spot. The soldier dropped his carbine to seize and detain the ladder, when a struggle ensued between him and the young officer for its possession.

At this critical moment, the soldier seeming to recollect himself, turned to raise his gun, either to shoot Selim or give the alarm; in either case it would be equally fatal to the success of their design. The boy had maintained his position during the brief struggle, but the moment the guard turned to recover his carbine, the half witted creature leaped from his high position directly upon his back and neck and bore him to the ground. The weight of the boy's body was sufficient to bring the soldier to the ground with stunning effect and leave him nearly insensible.

Had this not been the case the boy's finger clutched the throat with the power of a vice and the guard was as insensible as a dead man. In the mean time, the young officer scarcely knowing what to make of the opportune and sudden interference in his favor, drew up the ladder on the other side and prepared to follow Komel, who was already hurried by the Armenian nearly to the side of the boat that waited there, and in the stern of which sat another person in charge of the same. Komel looked back as she was joined by Captain Selim, and asked:

"Where is the boy?"

"What boy?" said the Armenian, ignorant as to whom they referred.

"The half-witted pet of the Sultan's."

"I left him in the grounds," said Selim. — "The guard passed over the ladder, but just as he was about to discharge his carbine, that boy sprang upon him like a tiger, and I think he must have killed him, for I saw the soldier lying on the ground insensible."

"That boy has been my best friend, I cannot bear to leave him."

"It would be madness to stop for anything now," replied the young officer; and so they passed around to the spot where the boat was in waiting, moored closed to the shore.

But let us look back for a moment at the scene on the other side of the seraglio wall where we left the guard overcome by the boy. The poor half witted child sat close beside the body, which was perfectly inanimate. Now he looked up at the bright stars for an instant, now at the still features of the guardsman, and then at the spot where the slave had disappeared over the wall. His movements were nervous and irregular, and he seemed to be trying to understand something or to make up his mind upon some thought that had stolen into his brain.

Suddenly he lifted his head, his eyes glowed like fire, and his chest heaved like a woman's. — He scanned the wall for an instant, then turning, retreated a few yards towards the centre of the grounds. With a short start and a wild bound he was upon its top! another leap carried him to the ground, and with the speed of a horse he ran to the water's edge, just in time for Komel to stretch out her hand and draw him on board the boat. He who sat in the stern was muffled up, and his face could not be seen, but he started to his feet at what seemed to him to be an intrusion; but a sign from the Armenian put all to rights, and the boy coiled himself up like a piece of rope at the feet of the fair girl.

Time was precious to them now, and Selim seizing one oar, the Armenian pulled with another, while he in the stern steered the caique quietly beneath the shade of the shore for some distance, when her course was suddenly altered, and striking boldly across the harbor, it was soon lost among the shipping at anchor.

A little adroitness, with cool courage, will often put all calculations at fault, and thus had the plan for Komel's release proved perfectly successful; thus had the Sultan been robbed of his favorite slave from out the very walls that encircled his palace grounds in spite of all his supposed security. Though it was very plain that the whole affair came very near miscarrying at the time when the guard appeared, and would perhaps have done so had the fellow understood his duty and fired a shot at once, thus if not shooting those engaged in this depredation upon the Sultan's household, at least giving an alarm that would probably have resulted in the arrest of all the parties concerned. But thanks to the bravery and skill of the poor half-witted boy, all had gone safely through, and now Komel found herself seated with the beautiful Zillah in Selim's cabin, safe from all harm.

"So," said the Armenian, drawing a long breath after the unusual exertion he had just experienced, "all is safe thus far. Now we must expedite matters for you to embark in your own craft at once, and in the mean time keep every thing close, especially the boy. He seems so devoted to the girl that it would be too bad to part them, but if he should be seen by any one he will be remembered, and it may lead to detection at once."

"That is true," answered Selim; "but we have got all on board without being observed even by the anchor watch."

"The Sultan will leave no means untried to detect the thief who has stolen his fairest jewel," said the Armenian, "and his reward will be so rich as to tempt the cupidity of every one, therefore be cautious and trust none."

"I will not. At midnight to-morrow we must be on board the Petrel, and at the most quiet moment slip her cable and drop quietly down the coast with the night breeze, and if every thing is propitious, we can get well away in the Black Sea before anything will be suspected of us, and pursuit instituted."

"I shall feel the utmost anxiety until you are fairly away," said the Armenian.

"We owe much to you," replied Selim.

Thus saying, the Armenian and Selim entered the cabin together, where Zillah and Komel sat listening to each other's stories, and fast coming to know each other better and better. Suddenly Komel turned to Selim, and after acknowledging how much she already owed him and the Armenian, said—

"There is one thing I meant to have asked you before."

"And what is that?"

"Who was it that sang that song beneath the seraglio walls?"

"The same notes that formed our signal to-night?" asked Selim.

"Yes."

"O, that was a young Circassian, who is on board here," was the answer.

"But judging from the song he sang, he must be from my native valley."

"Was it familiar to you?"

"As my mother's voice," answered Komel, with feeling. "It is a song that one most dear to me has sung to me many a time, and when a few nights since I heard it, I would have declared that it was his voice again; but I knew him to be gone to a better land; the Sultan took his life, alas! on my own account."

The Armenian looked at Selim, as much as to say, now for the surprise, while the young officer seemed hesitating as to what he should do next, when a noise was heard at the entrance of the cabin, and in a moment after, he who had steered the boat, slipped within and threw off the outer garment that had muffled him. All eyes were turned upon him as he stood for a moment, when Komel exclaimed, trembling as she said so:

"Is this a miracle, or do my eyes deceive me? that is—is—"

"Aphiz Adegah," said the Armenian, while an honest tear wet his cheek.

"Komel!" murmured the young mountaineer, as he pressed her trembling form to his breast.

All there knew their story, and could appreciate their feelings, while not a word was spoken, to break the spell of so joyous a meeting, the joy of such unhoped for bliss.

"The Sultan then deceived me," said Komel, suddenly recovering her voice.

"He was himself deceived, and thinks me dead," replied Aphiz; "my escape was miraculous."

"O, let us away at once from here," said Komel, anxiously; "the Sultan's agent will surely trace us, and I should die to go back to his harem again. Cannot we go at once?"

"Nay, have patience, my dear girl," said the Armenian, "our plans have been carefully laid, and we shall hardly run a single risk of detection or discovery if they are adhered to."

All this while, the half-witted boy lay coiled up in one corner of the cabin unseen, but himself noticing every movement that transpired, until as they all settled more quietly to a realizing sense of their relative positions, when Komel seeking him brought him to Aphiz, and told him how much she owed the poor boy for kindness rendered to her, and even that he had saved her life once, if not a second time, by his mastering the guard.

While the boy looked upon Komel as she spoke, his fine eye glowed with warmth and expression, but when Aphiz took his hand, and he turned towards him, that light was gone, like the fire from a seared coal, and the optics of the idiot were cold and expressionless.

CHAPTER XIV.

THE CHASE.

The reader will remember the fleet and beautiful slaver mentioned in an early chapter, when lying off the port of Anapa. The same clipper craft that had conveyed Komel away from her native shores, was destined, singularly enough, to carry her back again, for this was the vessel Selim had secretly purchased and prepared for his escape with his companions from the domain of the Sultan. He was too good a seaman not to manage affairs shrewdly, and though the coming night was the one on which he had resolved to sail, yet the schooner floated as lazily as ever at her moorings. The sails were closely trailed, and the ropes and sheets coiled away as though they would not be used for months again.

But could one have looked on board beneath her hatches, and out of sight of the crowded shipping in the bay, he might have counted a dozen stalwart youths, in the Greek costume, busily employed in getting everything ready below for a quick run, and as the shadows deepened over the Oriental scene, and the sun had fairly sunk to rest behind the lofty summit of Bulgurlu, one or two of the crew might have been seen quietly engaged here and there on deck, but their lazy, indolent movements, rather speaking of a long stay at their present anchorage than an idea of an early departure, and yet a true seaman would have observed that they were loosing everything, in place of making fast.

It was nearly midnight when Selim and his party, headed by Aphiz, left his own ship in a small caique, and quietly pulled with muffled oars, to the side of the schooner, which they boarded without hailing. She had been moored the day previous without the outermost of the shipping, and scarcely had the party got fairly on board, when she slipped her cable, and showing the cap of her fore-topsail to the gentle night air that set over the plains of Belgrade and down the Valley of Sweet Waters, gradually floated away, until by hoisting a few rings of the flying jib, her bows were brought round, and she slipped off towards the Black Sea unnoticed.

Not so much as the creaking of a block had been permitted to disturb the stillness, and now, when Capt. Selim felt too impatient not to make the most of the favorable land breeze, only the light jigger sail that was set so well aft as to reach far over the taffrail, was unfurled easily and dropped into its place, swelling away noiselessly. As impatient as he felt, he wished to skirt those shores silently, and resolved to take every precaution that would prevent a suspicion of the real hurry and anxiety that he felt from evincing itself.

The cutter hugged the Bithynian shore until it had passed that rendezvous for the caravans from Armenia and Persia, the favorite city of Scutari, and then it gradually approached the sea, its mainsail, foresail and topsails were spread, and before the first gray of morning broke over the horizon of the sea, the cutter had almost lost sight of the continent of Europe, and was swiftly ploughing the waves of the great inland ocean. Classic waters! laving the shores of Turkish Europe, Asia Minor, the broad coast of Russia, and that ancient island of Crimea, and finally washing the mountain coast of Circassia and Abrasia.

One of those short cross seas to which inland waters are so liable, was running at the time, and there were evidences, too, of foul weather, for the wind that sets from the north-east for three-fourths of the season in these waters, had hauled more westerly, and dark, ominous looking clouds obstructed the light of the sun as it rose from the horizon. The wind came in sudden and unequal gusts, now causing the clipper to careen till her topsail yards almost dipped, and then permitting her to rise once more to the upright position. Capt. Selim noted these signs well, for he knew the character of these waters, and that these signs prognosticated no favorable coming weather. His sails were first reefed, then close reefed, and finally furled altogether, save a fore-staysail, and the mainsail reduced to its smallest reef points.

While the clipper was scudding under this sail, a close lookout was kept in her wake, for Selim knew very well that at farthest his absence would only be concealed until the morning gun should fire, when the fleetest ship in the Sultan's navy would be dispatched to overtake him. And this was indeed the case, for just at this moment there came to his side a young Greek, who acted as his first officer, and pointing away astern in the south-western board, said:

"There is a man-of-war, sir, standing right in our wake hereaway."

"You are right—we are discovered, too, for he steers like a hawk on the wing about to dive for its prey."

"He is close handed, sir, while we are running nearly free."

"Then he has not yet made out the schooner's bearings; keep her as she is."

Watching the frigate, Selim still held on his course steadily, but the size of the enemy enabled her to carry twice the amount of canvass in proportion to her tonnage that he dared to do. Indeed, he felt the fleet craft under his feet tremble beneath the force with which she was driven through the water even now. As the morning advanced, the frigate gained fast upon them, until at the suggestion of Aphiz, the foresail, close reefed, was put upon the schooner, but quickly taken in again. It was too evident that the gale was increasing, as the bows of the schooner were every other minute quite under water, then she would rise on the next wave to shake the spray from her prow and side like a living creature, then boldly dash forward again.

"That fellow is in earnest," said Selim to Aphiz, "and is determined to have us, cost what it may. See, there goes his fore-to-gallant sail clear out of the belt ropes. Heaven send he may carry away a few more of sails, for he is overhauling us altogether too fast for my liking."

"There goes a gun," said Aphiz.

"Ay, fire away, my hearties," said Selim, "you lose a little with every recoil of that gun, and you can't reach us with anything that carries powder in the Sultan's navy—I know your points."

"That shot struck a mile astern of us," said Aphiz.

"Yes, and at the present rate, it will take him nearly two hours to overhaul us; but by that time, if the gale goes on increasing in this style, he must take in his canvass or lose his masts over the side."

Selim was right, the fury of the gale did increase, and he soon saw the frigate furl sail after sail for her own security, and yet she seemed under nearly bare poles to gain slowly on the schooner, and was now ranging within long shot distance, and commenced now and then to fire from her bow ports. But gunner, ever uncertain on the water, is doubly so in a gale, and nearly all her shot were thrown away, one now and then hitting the clipper, and causing a shower of splinters to fly into the air as though the spray had broken over the spot.

Chance did that for the frigate which all the skill of its gunner could not have done, and a shot aimed at her running gear took a slant upon the wave, and entered her side below the water line, causing a leak that was not discovered until it was too late to attempt its stoppage, and the schooner was slowly settling into the sea.

In the meantime the gale had reached its height, and the frigate, too intent on her own business, had long since ceased firing, and had dashed by the clipper like a race-horse, with everything lashed to the her decks and battened down. And now, when Selim discovered the extent of the danger, and realized that ere long the schooner must sink, he almost wished that the frigate, which had gone out of sight far down to leeward, might be seen once more.

Already had the schooner leaked so fast as to drive the occupants from the cabin to the quarter deck, and here, gathered in a small group, they looked at each other in silence, for death seemed inevitable.

"O, Selim! must we perish?" whispered his young and lovely Zillah.

"Dearest, I trust we may yet be saved. The gale will ere long subside, and even now we are drifting towards the very coast that we should have steered for had all been well with us."

This was so. The clipper, though gradually settling deeper and deeper into the sea, was yet propelled before the breeze by all the canvass that it was deemed prudent to place upon her, right towards the Circassian coast, at a rate perhaps of from four to five knots. The gale, too, now gradually subsided, and enabled the half-wrecked people to take more comfortable positions, and Aphiz and Selim to prepare a raft with the assistance of the crew, for it was but too apparent that the schooner must go down before long. Hollow groaning sounds issued from the hatches as she settled lower and lower, and it really seemed as though the fabric was uttering exclamations of pain at its untimely fate.

By unbinding and loosing the fore and main yards, a foundation was made by lashing these spars together, upon which other timbers and wood work was fastened, and in a few hours a broad and comparatively comfortable raft was formed. But how to launch it? That was beyond the power of all those on board united. To wait until the time when the water should float it from the deck, would be to run the risk of being engulfed with the schooner, and being drawn into the vortex of water that would follow her going down, and thus meet a sure and swift destruction.

But this was now their only hope, and the only means offering itself for their escape, since the stern and quarter boats had been lost or stove in the course of the late gale, and so making a virtue of necessity, they all gathered upon the centre of the raft that had been thus hastily constructed, and awaited their fate. Aphiz and Selim bound their respective charges to the raft by cords about their bodies, to prevent the possibility of their being washed from its unprotected flooring.

Already the water washed over their very feet, and now and then the schooner gave a fearful lurch, that caused all hands to stand fast and believe her going down. Gradually the water crept higher and higher, and the plunging schooner seemed at every fall of her bows to be going down. Even the gentle Komel and Zillah could understand the fearful momentary danger that must ensue when the hull should plunge at last, and they silently held each other's hands.

"Hurrah! hurrah!" cried one of the crew, at the top of his voice.

"What now?" demanded Selim sternly of the man, at his seemingly untimely mirth.

"She floats, she floats—the raft's afloat."

"Then in the name of Heaven, shove off as quickly as possible," said Selim, as he and Aphiz seize each an oar and strove to force the raft away from the deck. A way had already been cut through the bulwarks.

At first the raft did not stir, but gradually it slid away, and finally, to the joy of all, it was free and clear of the schooner's side, and by the strong efforts of the crew, they increased the space between them in a very few moments to the distance of several rods. It was not one moment too soon, for a deep gurgling sound rang on the ear for a moment, then the stern rose above the surface of the sea as the bows plunged, and in a moment after she was gone forever.

Even at a distance they had already gained, they felt the power of the vortex, and were drawn towards its brink with fearful velocity, as though they had been a mere feather floating upon the sea, but gradually the raft became once more steady, and as the twilight settled over the scene the whole party knelt in prayer for protection upon that wide, unbroken waste of waters.

They had taken the precaution to secure some food, though in a damaged state, and partaking sparingly of this as the moon lit up the wild scene, and the sea went down after its turmoil and tempest, they arranged themselves to sleep, Komel and Zillah close by each other's side, and the poor idiot boy coiled himself silently at their feet. He had been uncomplaining and watchful ever since the calamity, but had kept closer than ever to Komel's side, who, even in those moments of fearful trial, found time to bestow upon the boy looks and words of kind assurance, — that was enough — he seemed happy.

All the day and another night were passed thus. The fearful gale had cleared the sea of navigators, who had not yet ventured out from their safe anchorage, and still the raft drove on, aided by a little jury mast and the fore-topsail of the schooner, which had been hastily unbent and placed on the raft. Hunger had attacked them, for the provisions they had saved were now all gone, and this, added to the exposure they suffered, caused many a blanched cheek, and Komel and Zillah seemed ready to give way under the trial.

It was at the dawn of the third day that their eyes were gladdened by the distant hills of Abrasia, and soon after they neared the coast so as to make out its headlands, when a favoring wind, as if on purpose to speed them on their way, came over the Georgian hills from the south-east, and blew them towards the north.

Aphiz was now in a region that he knew well the navigation of, and he declared that with the wind holding thus for a few hours, they would be off the port of Anapa as safely as a steamboat might carry them.

This was indeed the case, and before many hours the well known hills and headlands of Circassia were visible to their longing eyes. Komel could not suppress the joyous burst of feeling that a sight of her native hills again infused into her bosom, but forgetting each pain and trouble, she pointed out first to Zillah, then to Aphiz, and even to the idiot boy, a beauty here, a well known spot there, and the hill behind which stood the cottage of her dear parents. O, how she trembled with impatient joy to reach its door once more.

Under the skilful guidance of Aphiz and Selim, the raft was steered into the harbor, and was soon surrounded by a score of boats, offering their ready assistance to relieve their distresses, and a short time after saw them landed safely, all upon the long, projecting mole.

All the while Selim seemed thoughtful and absent, and looked about him with strange interest, at everything that met his gaze. He even forgot to seek the side of Zillah, who, with Komel, was hurrying away to a conveyance up the mountain side. Nor did he join them until sent for by Aphiz.

Let another chapter explain the mystery of this singular abstraction.

CHAPTER XV.

HAPPY CONCLUSION.

The skies were yet blushing with departing day, and the evening shadows were quietly advancing over mountain top and sheltered valley, the dew was already touching the evening atmosphere with its fragrant mist, "Leaving on craggy hills and running streams, A softness like the atmosphere of dreams," when those who had so providentially been saved from the wreck, wended their way to the door of Komel's home. Scarcely could the poor girl restrain her impatience, scarcely wait for a moment to have the glad tidings broken to those within, before she should throw herself into her parents' arms. O, the joy that burst like sunshine upon those sad, half broken hearts, while tears of happiness coursed like mountain rivulets down their furrowed cheeks. Their dear, dear child was with them once more. Komel was safe, and they were again happy.

"But who are these, my child?" asked the father of Komel, pointing to Selim and Zillah.

"To him am I indebted, jointly with Aphiz, for my deliverance from bondage," she answered, taking Selim's hand and leading him to her father. "And this," she continued, putting an arm about Zillah, "is a dear sister whom I have learned to love for her kindness and sweet disposition. Both come to make our mountain side their future home."

Nor was the poor half-witted boy forgotten, but he received a share of the kindly welcome, and seemed in his peculiar way to understand and appreciate it, keeping continually by Komel's side.

An hour around the social board seemed to acquaint them all with the history of the past twelvemonth, and to reveal more than we might specify in many pages. The cottage was full of grateful hearts and happy souls that night; and Aphiz learned that since Krometz had fallen in that fatal encounter, the deed of the abduction had been fully proved upon him, and that so earnest were the feelings of the mountaineers in relation to the justice of Aphiz's conduct in that matter that he need fear no trouble concerning it. Thus assured, he too joined the home circle of his parents.

Captain Selim, with his bride, made Komel's house their home, but the young officer could not close his eyes to sleep. He rose with fevered brow and paced the lawn before the cottage until morning. Strange struggles seemed to be going on in his brain like a waking dream; he was striving to recall something in the dark vista of the past.

"You seem trouble this morning," said Komel's father, observing his mood. "Are you not well?"

"No, not exactly well," replied Selim; "indeed a strange dream seems to come over me while I look about me here—this mountain air, these surrounding hills, the distant view of the sea, have I ever seen these things before, or is it some troubled action of the brain that oppresses me with undefined recollections?"

"Come in and partake of our morning meal; that will refresh you," said the mountaineer.

"Thanks; yes, I will join you at once," he replied, but turned away thoughtfully.

With the earliest morning, Aphiz was again at the cottage and by Komel's side. O, how beautiful did she look to him now, once more attired in her simple dress of a mountaineer's daughter. No tongue could describe the fondness of his heart, or the dear truthfulness of her own expressive face when they met thus again. Their hearts were too full, far too full for words, and they wandered away together to old familiar scenes and spots in silence, save that their sympathetic souls were all the while communing with each other. At last they came to a spot from whence the lovely valley opened just below them, when suddenly Aphiz pointed to a projecting and dead limb of a tree far beneath them, and asked Komel if she remembered the scene of the hawk and dove.

"Alas! dear Aphiz, but too well. It was indeed an unheeded warning."

"But the dove is once more restored now, dearest, and we must look only for happy omens."

"I have seen so much of sadness, Aphiz," she answered, "that I shall only the more dearly prize the quiet peacefulness of our native hills."

"Thus too is it with me. A few months of excitement, toil, danger and unhappiness abroad, has endeared each spot that we have loved in our childhood still more strongly to me."

"Then shall good come out of evil, dear Aphiz, inasmuch as we shall now live content."

"Have you seen Captain Selim this morning, Komel?" he asked.

"Yes, and I fear he is ill, some heavy weight seems to be upon his heart."

"Let us seek him then, for we owe all to his manliness and courage."

As the twilight hour once crept over hill and valley, the evening meal was spread on the open lawn before the cottage, and when this was over, all sat there and told of the events that had passed, and each other's experiences, for the few past months, during which time Komel had remained a prisoner at the Sultan's palace. Of Selim, they knew only so much of his history as was connected with themselves, and he was asked to relate his story.

"Mine has been a life of little interest," he said, "save to myself alone. Of my birth and parentage I know nothing, and my earliest recollections carry me back to the period when I was a boy on board a Trebizond merchantman, at a time when I was just recovering from what is called the Asia fever, a malady that often attacks those who come from the north of the Black Sea to the Asia coast to live. This fever leaves the invalid deranged for weeks, and when he recovers from it, he is like an infant and obliged from that hour to cultivate his brain as from earliest childhood, and he can recall nothing of the past. Thus I lost the years of my life up to the age of eight or nine.

"I served in that ship until I was its first officer, and by good luck, having been once employed in one of the Sultan's ships as a pilot during a fierce gale, through which I was enabled, by my good luck, to carry the ship safely. I was appointed at once a lieutenant in the service, with good pay, and the means of improvement. The latter my taste led me to take advantage of, and in a short time I found myself in the command, where I was able to serve you."

"But you had no means whereby to learn of your birth and early childhood?" asked Komel's mother.

"None; I have thought much of the subject, but what effort to make in order to discover the truth as it regards this matter, I know not."

"Had you nothing about your person that could indicate your origin?"

"Nothing."

"Nor could the people with whom you sailed account for these things?" asked Aphiz.

"They said that I was taken off from a wreck on the Asia shore, the only survivor of a crew."

"How very strange," repeated all.

"You found nothing then upon you to mark the fact?" asked Komel's mother once more, sadly.

"Nothing—stay—there was an oaken cross upon my neck. I had nearly forgotten that; I wear it still, and for years I have thought it a sacred amulet, but it can reveal nothing."

"The cross, the cross?" they cried in one voice, "let us see it."

As he unbuttoned the collar of his coat and drew forth the emblem, Komel's mother, who had drawn close to his side, uttered a wild cry of delight as she fell into her husband's arms, saying:

"It is our lost boy!"

Words would but faintly express the scene and feelings that followed this announcement, and we leave the reader's own appreciations to fill up the picture to which we have referred.

Yes, Captain Selim, the gallant officer who had saved Aphiz's life, and liberated Komel from the Sultan's harem, was her own dear brother, but who had been counted as dead years and years gone by. Could a happier consummation have been devised? and Zillah, who loved Selim so tenderly before, now found fresh cause for joy, delight and tenderness in the new page in her husband's history.

Selim, too, now understood the secret influence that had led him to
bid so high for the lone slave he had met in the bazaar, the reason
why he had, by some undefined intuitive sense, been so drawn
towards her in his feelings, for the dumb and beautiful girl was his
unknown sister!

And again when he heard her name mentioned, for the first time, by
the Armenian physician, it will be remembered how the name rung
in his ears, awaking some long forgotten feelings, yet so indistinctly
that he could not express or fairly analyze them. The same sensations
have more than once come over him since that hour while they were
suffering together the hardships of the week, and the fearful scenes
that followed the gale they had encountered after the chase.

Aphiz and Komel loved each other now, as they never could have
done, but for the strange vicissitudes which they had shared
together. They had grown to be necessary to each other's being, and
even when absent from each other for a few hours, in soul they were
still together. And hand in hand, side by side, they still wandered
about the wild mountain scenery of their native hills. They had no
thoughts but of love, no desires that were not in unison, no
throbbing of their breasts that did not echo a kindred token in each
other's hearts. Life, kindred, the whole world were seen by them
through the soft ideal hues of ever present affection.

And when, at last, with full consent from her parents, Aphiz led
Komel a blushing bride to the altar, and Selim and Zillah supported
them on either side, how happy were they all!

Years pass on in the hills of Circassia as in all the rest of the world
beside. Sunshine and shadow glance athwart its crowning peaks, the
waves of the Black Sea lave its shores, its daughters still dream of a
home among the Turks, and the secret cargoes are yet run from
Anapa up the Golden Horn. The slave bazaar of the Ottoman capital
still presents its bevy of fair creatures from the north, and the
Sultan's agents are ever on the alert for the most beautiful to fill the
monarch's harem. The Brother of the Sun chooses his favorites from
out a score of lovely Georgians and Circassians, but he does not
forget her who had so entranced his heart, so enslaved his affections,
and then so mysteriously escaped from his gilded cage.

But as time passes on the scene changes—rosy-cheeked children
cling about Aphiz's knees, and a dear, black-eyed representative of

her mother clasps her tiny arms about his neck. And so, too, are Selim and Zillah blessed, and their children play and laugh together, causing an ever constant flow of delight to the parents' hearts.

There ever watches over them one sober, quiet eye—one whom the children love dearly, for he joins them in all their games and sports, and astonishes and delights them by his wonderful feats of agility. It is the half-witted creature, who had followed and loved Komel so well. As years have passed over him, the sun-light of reason gradually crept into his brain, and the poor boy saw a new world before him. His only care, his only thought, his constant delight seeming to be these lovely children.

The events of the past are often recurred to by Komel and her husband, around the quiet hearthstone that forms the united home of Selim, Zillah, and themselves, and the sun sets in the west, shedding its parting rays over no happier circle than theirs. Nor does Komel now regret that she was once the Sultan's slave.

As now he lays down his pen, let the author hope that he has won the kind consideration and remembrance of those who have read his story of THE CIRCASSIAN SLAVE.

THE END.

A SCRAP OF ROMAN HISTORY.

BY AN UNKNOWN POET.

In the olden days of Roman
  Grandeur, glory, wealth, and pride;
Once there came a might legion
From a vast and far-off region
  And this Roman power defied.
Naught could stay their devastations
  In the lands through which they came;
All the weeping supplications
Of the terror-stricken nations
  Could not quench these Vandals' flame.
Ah! most cruel were the invaders,
  Cruel their chastizing rods!
For their hearts were stone-like hardened,
These remorseless and unpardoned
  Foes of men and all the gods.
And at last they came with boastings
  To the gods' and learning's home;
Came with boasting, loud and merry,
Came, at last, unto the very
  Walls of proud, imperial Rome.
Ah! why did they not, in mercy,
  Spare the "Mistress of the World!"
Or, why did they not, when power
Sat on Roman wall and tower,
  Come, and bid their darts be hurled.
For the Romans' strength was broken.
  Gone, like light from darkness, now;
Now, when most that strength was need,
Strength was not;—there
  Weakness worse than Venla's vow.
Bearing all the outward semblance
  Of a firm and mighty hold,
Rome was inwardly as feeble
As a cemeteried people
  Changed into corruption's mould.
Ease, corruption, strife, dissension,
  Gaiety, licentious mirth,

The Circassian Slave

Luxury;—O, bane of mortals!
All had sapped the very portals
  Of this mightiest queen of earth.
Therefore, when these hordes of robbers
  Swarmed around the Roman's way,
Scarcely shadow of resistance
Met them near, or in the distance,
  And they found an easy prey.
Vandals, Alans, Allemanni,
  Longobardi, Avars, Moors,
Goths, Suevi, Huns, Bulgarians,
Overwhelming, rude barbarians
  Conquered Rome with deafening roars.
Desecrated, fired and plundered,
  Worse than vessel tempest-tost.
Rome was by her dissipations
Blotted from the list of nations;
  Rome was lost!—forever lost!

CPSIA information can be obtained at www.ICGtesting.com
Printed in the USA
BVOW08s1439100214

344494BV00001B/194/A